Shoot the Lawyer Twice

Michael Bowen

Poisoned Pen Press

Library of Congress Catalog Card Number: 2008923144

ISBN: 978-1-59058-529-0 Hardcover

Poisoned Pen Press
6962 E. First Ave., Ste. 103
Scottsdale, AZ 85251
www.poisonedpenpress.com
info@poisonedpenpress.com

Printed in the United States of America

For Anna Charlotte Sigmon, with all my heart

Disclaimer

This is a work of fiction. The events described did not take place and the characters depicted do not exist. They are products of the author's imagination. Any resemblance between characters and events in this novel and actual persons and events is coincidental and unintended. In short, don't kid yourself: you're not in here—I made this stuff up.

Acknowledgment

I would like to express my grateful appreciation for the assistance on certain technical matters of Dr. Brian Akers, an imaginative physician and a talented attorney.

Chapter One

On April 17, 2007 a federal grand jury in Milwaukee, Wisconsin indicted Jimmy Clevenger for piracy on the high seas. Clevenger thought he'd dodged the bullet when the Milwaukee County DA decided not to prosecute, but then this federal thing blindsided him.

Clevenger had always thought it would be kind of cool to be a celebrity—you know, fifteen minutes of fame, a little tube time, that kind of thing—but having Nancy Grace pronounce him guilty on CNN a week before his trial wasn't what he'd had in mind. His transcript at the University of Wisconsin-Milwaukee hadn't looked any too hot even before the indictment, and a felony conviction figured to mess up his resumé for sure. Plus, from everything he'd heard, prison could be a real bitch.

So, bottom line, in his opinion his situation pretty much sucked. And as for the people who died in the aftermath of his escapade—well, he felt bad about them, but the way he saw things that part wasn't really his fault.

PART ONE
Small Stakes

*"Academic politics is much more vicious than real politics
…because the stakes are so small."*

—Richard Neustadt

Chapter Two

Independence Day, 2005

"It's good we're here," Boone Fletcher said. "A July Fourth fireworks display is a traditional American community event."

"So's a lynching." As he spoke, Quintus Ultimusque Kazmaryk pointed at a moonlit figure slicing toward them through Lake Michigan. "She doesn't look drunk. Or he."

"I can't swim that well when I'm sober."

"When was the last time that happened?" Kazmaryk never let facts get in the way of a *mot juste*. Or even, as in this case, a *mot mediocre*.

Fletcher focused on the swimmer. He and Kazmaryk stood on a footpath about ten feet wide along the top of a breakwater arching a good half-mile from McKinley Marina toward Milwaukee's downtown shoreline. It was just after midnight, the lakefront fireworks now a memory to the hundred-thousand spectators trying to make their way home. Many of them no doubt glanced ruefully at the lake, envying the swells who'd watched the rockets and starbursts from ringside seats on cabin cruisers or sailboats and now had no crowds of surging humanity nor snaking ribbons of snarled traffic to fight.

"You think she's gonna have a problem?" Kazmaryck had decided that the swimmer was female.

"Could be."

The woman had to have covered more than a quarter-mile already—and this wasn't some suburban swimming pool. This was Lake Michigan, a churning, surging inland sea that in its time had swallowed ocean-going freighters without a burp and was now fouled with waste from abundant party boats as well as the usual flotsam and jetsam.

Kazmaryk dropped flat near the curving top of one of the ladders that rose from the water to the footpath every thirty feet or so along the breakwater. Easing his torso over the slight lip that edged the walkway, he stretched his two-hundred-twenty pounds of unevenly distributed bulk gingerly toward the water.

"What are you doing, you idiot?"

Fletcher asked this question for form's sake. He lay next to and slightly behind the older man, left hand gripping Kazmaryck's trouser belt and right hand prepared to brace himself against the walkway's lip if Kazmaryck suddenly surged forward. Within seconds wavelets washing over the breakwater soaked both of them from scalps to knees.

The swimmer seemed to notice them. The intensity of her strokes increased. Panting, sputtering, the young woman drew within ten yards, then five, and finally reached her sodden right arm out to Kazmaryk. He cursed in two languages as his hands slipped off at the first grab, then managed to grip her arm and guide her hand to the ladder. Swinging her legs under her like an expert while she anchored herself on the ladder and Kazmaryk's grip, she found footing on the ladder's lowest rung and climbed awkwardly onto the walkway. Fletcher expected to hear panic in her voice. He heard rage instead.

"He tried to rape me on my own boat!"

"Who's 'he?'" Fletcher took off his windbreaker and wrapped it around the shoulders of the shivering woman. "And who are you?"

The woman blinked at his blasé tone.

"Are you cops?"

"No. I'm a reporter, and Mr. Kazmaryk here makes his living operating a store on the south side and running for public office."

"Collectibles and keys-made-while-you-wait." Kazmaryk winked.

"Now who are you? And who tried to rape you?"

"My name is Carolyn Hoeckstra."

"What?" Kazmaryk yelped.

"Good poker face, Q."

"And the punk who came after me is Jimmy Clevenger."

When two detectives came to Clevenger's Oakland Avenue apartment at 6:45 that morning, the sleepy stoner who answered the door told them that Clevenger wasn't there. This was true. Clevenger was at that moment and for several hours afterward in the office of Walter Kuchinski, Esq., undergoing a withering interrogation by Kuchinski and one other attorney, who happened to have given birth to him some twenty years before.

He just didn't see what the fuss was. Yes, he and a bud had taken a Jetski out to some chick's boat because they'd been given to understand that there was some major fox action on board—as indeed there was, oh yes. Primo talent, my man. Someone had invited them on board. He couldn't remember who. Just a normal fireworks party, except only liquor and beer. No drugs, not even pot. He had *absolutely no idea, man,* why the Hoeckstra dudette suddenly dove overboard and swam desperately for shore.

"I mean, I swear, man. 'Sex or swim' is just an *expression.*"

Chapter Three

"Can I have one?" Rep Pennyworth reached for a brownie, just in case the answer were yes.

"No! Those are for the fleet!" Melissa swatted at her husband's grasping hand but missed as he prudently withdrew it. "How much of that manuscript have you read?"

"One page. The action starts with a character tailgating at the Meadowlands before a Giants game. Boilermakers are involved. By the bottom of the page he's headed for a Port-a-Potty."

"He's doomed. Appearing in the first sentence of a Taylor Gates thriller is an express ticket to eternity."

Rep skimmed the next pages of the typescript while Melissa wrapped the brownies in wax paper and then fitted them into an oblong cardboard box, over a layer of Rice Krispie treats.

"You're right. Page four. Some spoilsport has replaced the Lysol tablets at the bottom of the Port-a-Potty with cyanide capsules over an iron grid coated with sulphuric acid. When the poor schlub relieves himself his urine dissolves the capsules, the cyanide interacts with the acid, and hypocyanic gas is released, just like in a California execution back in the 'fifties."

"He tries to get out, of course." Melissa dabbed at a mailing label with a Sharpie. "But someone has locked the door from the outside and blocked the vent. In the moments before he passes out no one hears his strangled cries for help or his futile beating on the plastic walls of his macabre death chamber."

"Bingo."

"Kind of thing that happens every day at the Meadowlands."

"But how did you know? You couldn't possibly have read this yet. Amy Lee told me that this story is still being copy-edited. It isn't even in galleys yet."

"A Taylor Gates thriller is as predictable as the Harlem Globetrotters versus the Washington Generals," Melissa said. "It has a two word title. The first word is a noun. The first character on stage is a male who passes away in some gothic fashion before page ten. He doesn't get shot or stabbed or bludgeoned like a normal murder victim. He contrives instead to be guillotined, or transfixed by a harpoon, or defenestrated onto the fixed bayonets of soldiers conveniently presenting arms three stories below."

"Always a male, huh?"

Melissa sealed the box and taped a mailing label to it:

> *Any Midshipman*
> *c/o Command Chaplain*
> *Bancroft Hall*
> *United States Naval Academy*
> *Annapolis, MD 21402*

"The she-victim appears at the beginning of chapter two. Although she'll stumble into mortal peril several times, she'll be saved on each occasion by Kai Diamond, the omni-competent albeit psychologically troubled protagonist."

"Then what makes her a victim?"

"She will be violated or severely traumatized either by a non-white or by an Arab who is described as 'swarthy.' Or, in one interesting variation, by a panther. The latter is what we English professors call a metaphor."

"For interracial rape?"

"Yes. In the penultimate chapter the violator will pass away in grisly fashion at Diamond's hands."

"Even the panther?"

"You won't find any links to Taylor Gates on the PETA website."

"So Gates writes to a rather rigid formula."

"Gates writes with a cookie-cutter instead of a word-processor. He's a franchise. Picking up a Taylor Gates story is like ordering a Big Mac. You know exactly what you're going to get. The point isn't taste but predictability."

"That's what you English professors call an extended simile, isn't it?"

"Verging on Homeric. Why did Ms. Lee favor you with an advance peek at the latest entry in the Gates *oeuvre*?"

"She hinted at some legal business. No specifics, but even a small chance at Gates' contract and licensing work is worth some effort."

"I'm just glad you're getting paid for reading that stuff."

"I certainly wouldn't read it otherwise. Besides, you read pot-boilers on the job yourself. That's how you know so much about them."

"Sure. But I read them searching for profound links between sub-textual elements of American popular culture and socio-political constructs of race, class, and gender, so that I can write learned articles studded with arcane footnotes for abstruse academic journals."

"Well, I'm hoping that Lee and Gates will tell me what I'm searching for when they come to Milwaukee next month for the General Convocation of the Brontë Society of North America."

"Oops." Alarm flashed across Melissa's face, briefly distorting her expression. "The BSNA is meeting *here*?"

"So I gather. They'll be colliding with the sex-or-swim trial, but they scheduled it three years ago so their hotel rooms are safe. Why does that bother you?"

"Because the BSNA Convocation isn't just a fan convention, it's a Very Serious Scholarly Event. And if the Program

Committee finds itself short of properly credentialed Brontë scholars two weeks before the meeting they're going to ask the head of the English Department at a nearby university—"

"Namely, UWM."

"—namely UWM, to have some junior faculty member who can't say no whip up a little fifty-minute paper on short notice."

"You, for example."

"If I were any more junior I'd be running the Xerox machine."

"We copyright lawyers call those 'photocopiers,' by the way. If the event is so serious, what's a mid-list author of pot-boilers doing on a panel there? Gates has never even done historical fiction, has he?"

"Nope. He's been focusing on religious themes since *The Da Vinci Code* hit it big, but without showing any great concern for historical credibility. Few program chairs, however, can resist the temptation to add a little star power if they get the chance. After all, the Brontës wrote page-turners themselves."

"Well, thanks for the Cliff Notes. I feel ready for my final exam with Taylor Gates."

"All in a day's work, darling."

"The treats for the Naval Academy are Frank's idea, I take it?"

"Yes. My cherished older brother tells me that some of the mids' families can't get stuff like this to them for one reason or another. The chaplain uses these kinds of donations to even things up a bit."

"You've spent your morning well."

"Better than Taylor Gates spent his, in all probability," Melissa said. "But that's a pretty low bar."

Chapter Four

The second Thursday in August, 2007

When talking to assistant deans Melissa made it a point to stay in motion. She was doing so now and it was working. Assistant Dean René Cyntrip Mignon had been speaking for two minutes as he puffed along beside her through the basement maze at UWM's Curtin Hall, and so far her head hadn't exploded.

"I know there must be an explanation," Mignon panted, "but one of your summer mini-course students, Anne-Marie Cecil, claims that you used the term 'lesbian rule' in class in a, ah, disparaging sense."

"I did."

"I see. Well. That is unfortunate on so many levels. She found the term offensive, and is sure that members of the university's gay/lesbian/bisexual/ transgender community did as well. You see the difficulty."

"I certainly do. Ms. Cecil didn't do her homework."

"That's not exactly my meaning. You see—"

"As I'm sure you know, Dean, the first recorded use of the word 'lesbian' in English with reference to sexual orientation occurred in the late nineteenth century."

"To be frank, I don't think I did know that."

"I was being polite."

"My point, however, is—"

"The term 'lesbian rule,' by contrast, goes back to the Middle Ages. It refers to a measuring stick made of lead so that it could be bent around curved surfaces. By extension, it was used in theological disputation to mean a principle flexible enough to be bent opportunistically to support whatever position suited the speaker."

"I suppose so, but—"

"Which Ms. Cecil would have known if she had read the annotated correspondence of Thomas More, as my syllabus prescribed. Having failed to do so, she managed to find offense in a term that couldn't reasonably offend anyone except the Protestant theologians whom More accused of applying a lesbian rule to scriptural interpretation."

"To be sure," Mignon gasped, "but one can't expect the typical undergraduate to know that."

"I understand my responsibilities at this university to include teaching undergraduates things they don't know."

As they pelted up a broad set of stairs, the shade on Mignon's ballooning cheeks blossomed from vermillion to purple. Melissa decided that purple was one of her favorite colors.

"Without, however, transgressing the norms of our institutional mission, which include avoiding offensive statements. And if a statement *offends* someone, Professor Pennyworth, it is 'offensive,' no?"

The smirk Mignon offered seemed deliberately calculated to offend.

"'Niggardly,'" Melissa said.

The smirk evaporated, for Mignon vaguely recalled a kerfuffle over 'niggardly' a few years back, with everyone from Ruth Dudley Edwards to the *Washington Post* making fun of the confused activists who had exploded in shrill indignation over the word.

"I can't teach a course on Polemics as Literature without Thomas More," Melissa said then, "whereas I can very easily teach it without Ms. Cecil. I'm not going to dumb down More's muscular prose simply because it offends students who are too lazy to do the required reading. If she doesn't want to be offended she can either drop the course or do her homework."

"They are *so* young." Mignon's expression approached Dickensian pathos. "To the extent unintended and even unreasonable offense was taken, I would suggest a dignified apology."

"Ms. Cecil doesn't need to apologize; she just needs to read the assigned material."

"I, uh, meant that you might apologize to Ms. Cecil."

Thinking that she must have misheard him, Melissa stopped and stared at Mignon in unfeigned astonishment. Three seconds of scrutiny convinced her that she had understood him correctly.

"I'm afraid that is out of the question."

"I *am* the Assistant Dean of the Office of Inclusiveness Concerns."

Which means your mouth is writing checks your job description can't cash.

"As any apology would be insincere, I couldn't offer one without applying a lesbian rule. Have a pleasant day."

Melissa hustled up the next flight of stairs, confident that Mignon wouldn't follow her even if he could—which, at the moment, looked like a shaky proposition. She approached the printer/copier room that informally demarcated the History sector of Curtin Hall's Humanities and Social Studies Department from its English counterpart. Two plastic bins, one bright blue and the other bright green, sat on the floor outside the room. Although she couldn't read them yet, she knew that a hand-lettered sign on the blue bin read WHITE PAPER while the sign on the green one read COLORED PAPER.

Squatting in front of the green bin and hard at work with a felt tip pen was Tereska Bleifert, a soon-to-be sophomore who earned part of her tuition as a student aide in Humanities. Melissa had pulled to within five feet before Bleifert finally heard her footsteps and looked up, startled and flustered. Melissa glanced down. Bleifert had drawn an X through COLORED PAPER and inserted PAPER OF COLOR.

"Busted." Bleifert rose and sheepishly avoided Melissa's gaze.

"Convent school girls don't snitch," Melissa said, tapping her own chest.

"So you're not upset about my little, ah, gesture?"

"The only thing I'm upset about is that I didn't think of it first."

Melissa regarded Beleifert as a refreshingly old-school student—the kind of working class kid who belonged at this blue-collar, urban university. She often affected a casual cynicism that couldn't mask her youthful delight at finding herself at last among people as interested in learning as she was. In a course last spring on The Romantic Breakthrough she had come across as widely if not deeply read, but without the jaded, been-there-done-that attitude of North Shore brats from toney prep schools who were here instead of UW-Madison because they'd loafed their way to easy Bs instead of bothering with AP classes.

"I'm glad you ran into me, actually," Bleifert said. "You're like number five on a seven-item to-do list I have from Professor Angstrom, and since I missed lunch I'm kind of fiending for a Marb. Wait a minute, that came out a little lame, I guess."

"On the contrary, I can scarcely imagine a more flattering tribute than receiving priority over a cigarette break."

"Whatever. Let's see." Bleifert gravely consulted her PDA. "Oh, yeah. He was wondering if you might know any document examination experts who read Italian."

"Afraid not. My husband might. I'll make a note to ask him. Wait a minute. Assistant Dean Mignon may qualify. Italian is one his languages, and doesn't he teach Comparative Religious Studies? Ancient documents probably come up quite a bit in that field."

"If he ever taught, that's what he'd teach," Bleifert said, sounding more like the faculty lounge than the quad. "But he can't get any students for his courses even though they're easy A's, and he hasn't had a peer-reviewed publication in like, seven years. I don't think he'll make the short list."

A tingle of excitement tickled Melissa's gut as she recognized a teachable moment. A full year's experience on a university faculty apparently hadn't completely destroyed her pedagogic instincts.

"*English Bards and Scots Reviewers,*" she said.

"Byron. ' I awoke to find myself famous.'"

Through a closed door ten feet away Melissa heard her office phone ring.

"Come have your Marlboro in my office while I take that call. The cigarette police can't get you there. No ashtrays though, so be careful. I'm an accommodator but not a facilitator."

Followed by Bleifert, Melissa entered her office and caught her phone before the end of the third ring. The caller was Cynthia Stratton, a Michigan classmate now teaching at one of the Loyola Universities dotting the country. Melissa tried to remember whether it was Baltimore, Chicago, or Los Angeles.

"I just saw some galleys being circulated by *GRAIL*," she said. "Your little *Shrimp and Breach* piece has made Stanley Conger cross. 'Over-written, under-thought, and affectedly iconoclastic.' Congratulations."

"Thanks. He's breaking the first rule of academic writing: Never argue in public with anyone less important than you are."

"Now that I've buttered you up, I'll tell you why I called. Are you familiar with the Brontë Society of North America?"

"'Brontë.'" Melissa said the word slowly and elaborately, as if it were an obscure Babylonian term for some type of armor worn by Gilgamesh.

"BSNA is holding its General Convocation in Milwaukee this year. The theme is 'Use and Abuse of Religion in Brontë Text and Subtext.'"

"You know, Cindy, it's quite disgraceful but I have trouble keeping Charlotte and Emily straight."

"Um, 'Lissa? Hello? You wrote your master's thesis on the tension between environmental determinism and deconstructionist theory in *Wuthering Heights.*"

"Well, technically, that's true."

"Gotcha."

"Busted. I'm sorry, Cindy, but I simply don't have time to gin up a conference presentation in the next few weeks."

"Good, because that would be a conflict of interest. I want you to read a paper I've written that I've just learned I won't be able to give."

"That I can handle," Melissa said with vast relief.

"There are Power Points."

"I eat Power Points for breakfast. What's your topic?"

"'Charlotte Brontë's Anti-Catholicism: Victorian Conformity or Subliminal Obsession?'"

"I pick subliminal obsession. It's sexier."

"Just read the paper, professor. Now report to detention and write one-hundred times, 'I must not fib to my friends.'"

"You're letting me off easy. Send me the paper as soon as you can."

She hung up and turned toward Bleifert, who was standing near the far corner with her eyes politely averted, thoughtfully blowing smoke toward the ceiling vent and flicking ash into the wastebasket. Bleifert glanced around.

"Has *Peel and Eat Shrimp and Material Breach* sparked controversy?"

"It has earned me a blast in the *Graduate Review of Academic and Interdisciplinary Literature*, from someone who should know better."

"Good for you. I'm still working on Byron."

"He became an overnight celebrity by savaging half the poets in two countries. Do you think anyone would read *English Bards* today if he'd just done riffs on Addison or Swift instead of using his own voice?"

"I'm guessing no."

"If you want to lampoon a professor or a dean, including me, be my guest. Invective has a very respectable pedigree in English literature. But skewer us with your own sword. Don't parrot something you heard from Professor Angstrom."

"Point taken." Bleifert combined a becoming blush with a shy smile. "Thanks."

"Hey, I get paid to do this."

"You're not like a lot of professors. On most things you're skeptical about both sides but open to both. But on a few big things you can be downright dogmatic. You would have made a good Benedictine abbess."

"I don't think agnostics are allowed to be abbesses, even these days."

"It's none of my business, but 'agnostic' as in atheist-lite or as in you really don't know?"

"The latter. It isn't any of your business, but why stop an interesting conversation on a technicality?"

"The thing is, a good abbess is agnostic in just that sense. Not knowing is the essence of faith. Accepting the second law of thermodynamics isn't a matter of faith. If you truly know something, it isn't faith to believe it."

"A provocative thought." Melissa noticed a fierce, intensely focused gleam in Bleifert's eyes. It struck her as the kind of spark you might have seen in the eyes of a martyr on her way to the stake—or of a suicide bomber on his way to a crowded bus stop.

"I wasn't eavesdropping," Bleifert said then, her tone suddenly conversational again, "but I couldn't help hearing part of what you said during your phone call. It sounds like you and Dean Mignon will be on the same panel at the Brontë thing. That could get interesting."

"I'll just be reading a colleague's paper."

"Even so."

"Anything else, or did you just want to finish your cigarette?"

"One more thing, actually. You said your husband is a lawyer. If I had a question about that big trial that's coming up—the one they call the sex-or-swim case—do you think it would be okay if I asked him? I don't mean just idle curiosity, I mean something important."

"I'm not sure, but the quick way to find out is to ask him. If he can't talk about it he won't be shy about telling you. Here, let me give you his card."

"Thanks." Bleifert accepted the proffered card, put her cigarette out against the inside of Melissa's wastebasket, and re-shouldered her bulging, puce backpack. "You really have been very thoughtful. I appreciate it."

"You're quite welcome." Melissa smiled, both surprised and inwardly warmed by the almost stunningly retro good manners.

As soon as Bleifert had gone Melissa typed a quick email to Mignon, suggesting that he give Angstrom a call about examining an Italian document. A nanosecond after she'd hit SEND, though, she felt misgivings—a bit like the feeling she had when she played gin rummy with her dad and realized an instant too late that he'd somehow suckered her into dumping the very card he needed.

Chapter Five

The Third Wednesday of August, 2007

"What's a 'work made for hire?'" Harald Angstrom asked Rep.

"It's a creative effort produced by someone employed for the purpose by someone else, instead of working on his own. Hallmark Cards verses or advertising jingles, for example. The employer has the copyright and creative control. It's a good term for creative parties to keep out of their contracts."

"In my case, unfortunately, it's already there."

"Is the contract with the university?"

"It's with Goettinger Corporation." Angstrom brushed disgustedly at invisible specks on his blue denim work shirt. "A corporate history to commemorate the company's centennial in 2009."

"And someone at Goettinger doesn't like what you've written?"

"Well, they probably wouldn't like it if I'd written anything, but so far I haven't."

"Clio is a fickle muse."

"Nothing so pretentious as that. Ninety percent of writing history is gathering and organizing data. The key-punching itself goes quite fast. I just haven't quite gotten to that part yet."

"Have you missed any interim deadlines?"

"Strictly speaking I've missed every interim deadline. But one generally does in what some of my nastier colleagues call the history-whore business. Besides, Tim Goettinger keeled over in a confessional at Saint Josephat's more than two years ago and they haven't gotten around to naming an alternative contact yet. So I have a technical excuse."

"They're getting a bit restive, though, are they?"

"They want to cancel the whole project."

"Without paying you?"

"On the contrary, they'll let me keep the advance and they'll throw in the progress payment that would be due when I submitted the first draft. Fifty-thousand altogether just to tear up the contract."

"I'll try to phrase this next question as delicately as I can," Rep said, thinking of clients who didn't know what a progress payment was and would count themselves very lucky indeed to clear fifty-thousand for a completed work. "Why didn't you say 'yes' before their mouths were closed?"

"Because I want to write the book."

"I see."

"I haven't been entirely idle. I've gotten into the archives and found a rather provocative little story. This wouldn't be just a handsomely bound corporate valentine. It could turn into a passably decent work of local history."

"But only if you have creative control."

"Right."

Rep shrugged.

"If it's that important to you, no law says you have to take Goettinger's money. Treat their proposal as an anticipatory breach, return the advance, and write whatever you want. The advance part might be a hardship, but—"

"It would be an impossibility. Long since spent. I'm a fifty-seven-year old divorced professor still making monthly payments on half-a-duplex in Shorewood. Nothing about my Marxism is more sincere than my net worth. Put my IRA, my modest equity, and my 1999 Neon together and I couldn't come up with ten-thousand dollars, much less twenty-five."

"That sheds a different light on Goettinger's offer. To be cold-bloodedly realistic about it, why don't you take the money and run?"

"Let's just say the objective and subjective conditions of proletarian consciousness have converged." Angstrom's blue eyes glinted under bushy gray eyebrows. His coffin-plate smile suggested that there was only one cold-blooded realist in the room, and it wasn't Rep. "No doubt I can be bought. But not for fifty-thousand dollars."

"An important piece of self-knowledge."

"When I got my first tenure-track position almost thirty years ago, I was on cloud nine. Actually getting tenure ten years later brought transports of elation. *I could be a scholar! I could teach and write!*"

"But then reality intruded?"

"Reality kicked the door down and walked off with everything that wasn't nailed down. I started noticing students who'd gotten Cs from me driving BMWs on Downer Avenue, and waltzing into Midwest Airlines' pricey Best Care Club at the airport while I waited out flight delays at the gate with howling three-year olds and sales reps talking on cell-phone head sets."

"In other words, you didn't have much money."

"I had hardly any money at all. I don't mean I had to vacation in Wisconsin Dells instead of Acupulco. I mean I found myself sweating winter gas bills. We scholars don't do badly at the beginning but we hit the ceiling way too soon. So I've moonlighted a bit: appraisals of book collections, a couple of those vanity press institutional valentines, and some other things here and there to keep me in suede elbow patches."

"I get the picture." Rep paused for a moment as he tried to come up with the right lawyerly spin. "You feel that if you abandoned the Goettinger project for fifty-thousand dollars you'd be selling out."

Angstrom's soup-strainer moustache hid a smile even thinner than the last one.

"I sold out a long time ago, counselor. Now we're just negotiating."

"Negotiating can be an expensive hobby. What's the maximum you could get under the contract?"

"Two-hundred-fifty-thousand, unless Goettinger's bullying induces hysterical quadriplegia and we throw a little mental and emotional distress into the mix."

"Contract law doesn't work that way, and hysterical quadriplegia would be way past my choke point even if it did."

"I've stumbled over the last squeamish lawyer in America. So a contingent fee is out of the question?"

"Yes. To take litigation on spec my partners back in Indianapolis would insist on a six-figure upside for the firm and a slam-dunk on liability."

"That's the problem with capitalism. It's never really ruthless when you need it to be. Any ideas?"

"One. We can tell Goettinger that you're going to proceed with research among its customers, competitors, and present and former employees, and then pursue independent publication. You will hold them responsible for any loss in the benefit of your bargain."

"What will that accomplish?"

"If we're very, very lucky," Rep said, "it will get you sued."

"For breach of contract?"

"For everything under the sun, including things covered by your homeowner's insurance policy. Then your insurer will end up paying my bills."

"Suppose the insurer denies coverage?"

"That one we'd take on spec. When good lawyers die they spend eternity in heaven suing insurance companies."

"You'd take that case on the come even though your fees might not reach the magic six-figure level?"

"We'd see to it that they did."

"You're not so squeamish after all. How fast can you write the letter?"

Chapter Six

Three hours later Melissa reviewed with a mixture of dismay and bemusement a memorandum that Mignon had just circulated:

From: Professor René C. Mignon, Assistant Dean/ Office of Inclusiveness Affairs
To: Academic/Administrative Personnel
Re: Vandalism/Protest
Date: August 15, 2007

It has come to the attention of the University Office of Inclusiveness Affairs that, last week, a notice on a Curtin Hall repository reading "Colored Paper" was traduced to read "Paper of Color." If this was someone's idea of a joke, this Office does not think it was very funny. On the contrary, it was racist, hateful, and a violation of the core principles for which this university stands. If, on the other hand, one or more members of the University Community who are diverse found the sign offensive and altered it to protest insufficient sensitivity to minority concerns and an inadequate commitment to inclusiveness, then on behalf of the entire University Community this Office sincerely apologizes.

RCM

Melissa was trying to decide whether misuse of "traduced" was more alarming than the diction error lurking in "who *are* diverse" when she heard a knock.

"Do you have a minute, professor?" Mignon asked.

"It's too late to say no."

Mignon interpreted this as an invitation to sit down.

"I wanted to speak about your email concerning Professor Angstrom."

"I thought you might be able to help him."

"I might, but I'm afraid he's not interested in my assistance."

"That's regrettable, but I'm not sure what I can do about it."

"I was wondering whether you might be willing to tell Professor Angstrom that you could in fact arrange a translation and examination of the document, perhaps through some contact of your husband's. I can find the funds to pay for it, if there's a charge, as long as I can get a look at the thing myself. By functioning as a kind of honest broker, you would be doing a larger favor than you know not only for Angstrom but for the entire university."

"'Honest' strikes me as an odd way to describe lying to a colleague."

"Ordinarily, of course, I wouldn't suggest such a course."

"I should hope not."

"But extraordinary concerns are involved here."

"For example?" Melissa folded her arms across her chest and leaned back in her chair.

"I have spent almost two years trying to arrange a conference here on the role of Pope Pius the Twelfth in the Second World War."

"That's not exactly virgin territory, is it? It's not my field, but I have the impression that a spate of books on the subject hit the market a few years ago, and many of them are now viewed professionally as overhyped. Could a symposium here contribute something new and interesting?"

"Well that's just it, you see. You've put your finger right on it."

"I'm glad I've accomplished something in the last five minutes."

"One of Professor Angstrom's remunerative sidelines is appraising books of claimed historical value. His appraisals are always generous and word gets around. Donors seek him out, pay his fee, give the books to some worthy recipient, take a large tax deduction, and hope the IRS has more important things to worry about."

"All right." Melissa's temples began to pulse, and she wished that they were walking briskly across the quad right now instead of sitting in her office.

"Recently, Professor Angstrom provided such an appraisal for a set of nineteenth century Slavic hymnals supposedly given by the abbot of a monastery to an American officer to thank him for the consideration he and his men showed when they were billeted at the monastery in the closing weeks of the Second World War. The officer was from a prominent Milwaukee family, which held onto the hymnals as keepsakes. Now the family is going to donate the hymnals in the officer's memory to Villa Terrace—the decorative arts museum where some of the Brontë panels will be held."

"Including your panel?"

"Including mine, as it happens. The museum will officially thank the family the night of my panel."

"Where does the pope come in?"

"Angstrom has been hinting that he found a potentially surprising document from the early 'forties stuck in the pages of one of the hymnals. He has implied that it's a written order to the monastery to shelter Jews."

"You'd hardly expect monks to use something like that as a bookmark."

"The theory is that the abbot's gift of the hymnals was a cover for getting rid of what might turn out to be a compromising document if fascists ended up running Czechoslovakia after the war—something that certainly wasn't out of the question in early 1945."

"Seems a bit thin." Melissa put her forearms on her desk in an effort to make her posture seem less hostile. "In fact, the whole things sounds like a tease. I think Professor Angstrom may just be having fun with…people."

"But if it *is* true, you see, it's enormous." Mignon's voice vibrated with excitement. "It would be the only extant *written* order from the pope about helping the Jews."

"I can see the potential historical importance."

"It could be the centerpiece of a major symposium! Draw the top names in the field! Real star power! Heavy hitters!"

"Yes, that too, I suppose."

Apparently sensing the irony in Melissa's comment, Mignon came back down to earth. He gathered himself into the admixture of supplicant and bully peculiar to deanship.

"Will you, at least, consider it?"

"Yes, I will consider it," she replied

Melissa took what comfort she could in the reflection that this was not, technically, a lie. She would consider lying to Angstrom, compromising her integrity, and letting herself be used as a pawn in a grubby little game of academic politics, all in the name of some higher scholarly purpose. But when she was through considering it, she knew what the answer would be.

If I'm going to have a guilty conscience, I'll have a lot more fun getting it than this cheap little exercise would produce.

Chapter Seven

The third Monday in September, 2007

"Start with this."

A Marine officer in civilian clothes, Rep thought as the visitor handed him a synopsis of the next action/adventure novel moving down the Taylor Gates assembly line. Square-jawed. Direct gaze from no-nonsense eyes. Compactly muscular upper body. Erect posture. Exactly what you'd expect from the author of Kai Diamond's adventures.

Except that the speaker handing Rep the document wasn't Taylor Gates but his agent, Amy Lee. Gates himself, sitting beside her, was two inches taller than Rep but eighty pounds heavier. Flab flopped over the open collar on his shirt, and nothing about his upper arms suggested that he'd completed an obstacle course any time recently.

"'*Curia Code*,'" Rep read aloud from the first page of the synopsis. "'A thriller about papal politics in the very heart of the Vatican.'"

"*Not* a conspiracy to rig the election of the next pope." Gates wagged his finger and shook his head to reinforce this pronouncement. "That's been done. This story is a *lot* edgier."

"Does the first character to appear get hacked to death by Swiss Guards?"

"Too clichéd. He's poisoned by curare secreted on the inside of his condom."

"No need to tell me more, especially since you'd probably have to kill me if you did."

Gates, however, couldn't help himself. Ignorning Lee's frown, he leaned forward, almost trembling with delight.

"A plot to fix the canonization of a saint. Not some martyr from the Dark Ages. A twentieth-century figure—and a very controversial one. The marketing strategy comes from *The Hunt for Red October*. We want to get the idea out that the story is based on events that are actually happening—and we have a line on *that*, too."

"It's an atomic bomb," Lee said.

Saint Robert Oppenheimer? Rep managed to stifle these unconstructive words before they passed his lips.

"It sounds very promising."

"Oh, it's *promising* all right." Gates' voice-box seemed to be equipped with an automatically functioning italics key.

"Religious thrillers have been very hot ever since *Angels and Demons* and *The Da Vinci Code*," Lee explained. "It's becoming a very crowded field."

"We're positioning Kai for counter-programming," Gates said. "Thirty-two percent of the people who buy at least one mystery or thriller a month are practicing Catholics, mostly over forty-five. They tend to be more conservative than other segments of the genre demographic. They go to church more often, vote Republican, own guns, and buy American."

"Which means there's a huge potential market for someone who can come off as the anti-Dan Brown," Lee said. "A religious thriller that's pro-God instead of anti-Catholic. We won't be Pepsi to his Coke but Gatorade to his Hawaiian Punch."

"Prius Hybrid to his Oldsmobile Eight-eight," Gates interjected.

"Nicorette to his Winstons," Rep murmured.

"*Exactly*." The Gates italics button functioned with its customary efficiency.

It occurred to Rep that Dan Brown might have found this assessment less than fair and balanced. But Dan Brown wasn't proposing to hire him, so he kept his mouth shut. The resulting silence didn't last long enough to be uncomfortable, for Lee immediately filled it.

"We've got the inside track because of *Mission Creep*, the story I sent you last month. But there are lots of thriller wannabes out there trying to mine this vein and looking for buzz."

"Capitalism can be a bitch." Rep glanced from Lee to Gates and back again. "What do you need from me?"

"Look at this."

Lee worried an oversized, oxblood leather legal pad holder out of an undersized, oxblood leather envelope briefcase. Then, with a deliberate solemnity that verged on liturgical, she opened the holder, eased a printed page from the flap inside, and handed it to Rep.

Rep looked down at a photocopy of a spring, 2005 article apparently taken from the *Milwaukee Journal Sentinel* and printed off the internet:

Local Industrialist Dies at St. Josephats

Milwaukee industrialist and business leader Timothy Goettinger died of an apparent heart attack at St. Josephat's Basilica yesterday afternoon, while confessions were being heard. Responding to an unidentified 911 caller, EMTs found Mr. Goettinger's body inside one of the confessionals. One bystander said that she was drawn to the confessional, which was not in use, when she noticed a mist seeping from underneath the door.

EMT Fred Norman said that Goettinger was already dead when the response team arrived, approximately seven minutes after the 911 call. He said that the misting substance was apparently carbon monoxide from an industrial cylinder found near the body. Norman said that carbon monoxide poisoning was not the cause of death, but declined to specu-late about whether the gas played any role in what happened.

Goettinger was president and CEO of Goet-tinger Corp., a machine tool manufacturer that has had its headquarters on Milwaukee's south side since 1909. The company was in the news recently as a result of a federal investigation into alleged improper payments to foreign officials in connection with the sale of CNC lathes. No charges were ever brought.

Goettinger is survived by his daughter, Carolyn Goettinger Hoeckstra, 25, and his son, Henry "Hank" Goettinger, 22. Goettinger was 58.

"Carbon monoxide in church?" Rep asked after he'd finished reading the piece. "I've only been in Milwaukee since last year, but even so I'm surprised I haven't heard about something as off-the-wall as this."

"You haven't heard about it because it didn't happen." Lee twitched impatient fingers at Rep, who obediently returned the clipping. "At least not the way it's recounted here. Someone went to a lot of trouble using Printshop or something to set this local story up in *Journal Sentinel* typeface and font, insert stuff about lethal gas that echoes *Mission Creep*, and send it anonymously to Taylor last month."

"A pretty elaborate hoax," Rep said.

"Or a pretty clumsy threat." Gates accompanied this assess-ment with a Meaningful Look that evoked 'sixties-era private eyes.

"Who would want to threaten you?"

"Someone who'd like to be first on the anti-*Da Vinci Code* bandwagon and therefore wants me to jump off."

"Possible. But a matter for cops rather than lawyers, no?"

"Whoever did this obviously had access to the *Mission Creep* storyline," Lee said.

"Apparently."

"Which means we have a leak."

"That would follow."

"And a very strong possibility that the leaker is working with someone in or near Milwaukee, because who else would have noticed this story?"

"Fair enough." Rep hoped that Lee was approaching an answer to this question. She was.

"In the synopsis of *Curia Code* that I gave you at the beginning of this meeting, we don't identify Taylor as the author and we don't call the protagonist Kai Diamond. We'd like you to shop the synopsis around to a list of editors that I'll give you. Pitch it as the work of one of your clients, whom you won't identify until there's a strong expression of interest."

"What will that accomplish?"

"There will be…*reactions*," Gates rumbled.

"Which will tell us what we need to know."

Rep considered the pair in front of him, who each seemed serenely unaware that their proposed assignment raised more ethical issues than a professional responsibility symposium for lawyers in New Jersey.

"I'm not a literary agent. I'm a lawyer."

"A lawyer is just an agent with malpractice insurance."

Rep had to smile. Lee had him there.

He listened with respectful but distracted attention while she talked about paying his standard hourly rate and hinted about "more conventional legal work down the road." He wasn't tempted. A client who'll ask his lawyer to lie will lie to his lawyer. Besides, this was out of the question. That was easy. The more challenging part would come when Lee finally ran out of steam, which she seemed on the verge of doing.

"So. Can we do this?"

"Never ask a lawyer what you can or can't do. Ask him how to do what you want to do."

"Okay," Gates rasped, "how can we smoke the leaker out?"

"I don't know. I'll try to come up with something that won't land you in court or me in front of a bar disciplinary committee. I'd like to meet with you again in a couple of weeks or so."

"Easily done," Lee said. "We'll be at the Pfister Hotel. We decided to come in a little early for the Brontë thing and we'll be staying there."

"I'm surprised you were able to get rooms downtown. We have a big trial starting soon that the media are calling the sex-or-swim case. I thought reporters had soaked up every room south of Sheboygan for the duration."

"It's all in knowing how to ask." Gates' voice made Rep think of condoms and curare.

Chapter Eight

The first Thursday in October, 2007

Rep figured he'd never see anything more dramatic in a court-room than the jury returning its verdict in the sex-or-swim case. If the world had ended three minutes later, he would have been right.

He and Angstrom watched the show from seats just behind the bar, next to Goettinger Corporation's lawyers. As Rep had hoped, his letter had baited the company into suing Angstrom. Word that the sex-or-swim jury finally had a verdict interrupted a humdrum scheduling conference in Angstrom's case, so they were able to grab choice seats before the reporters and other spectators rushed in to hear the verdict read.

From no more than eight feet away he saw thousand-dollar suit coats strain against shoulders as Clevenger and his lawyers tensed. After taking the verdict form back from a poker-faced judge, the clerk pulled a sleek, black tube close to her mouth.

"United States v. Clevenger, case number 07-CR-103. On the charge of willfully boarding a vessel on the high seas for the purpose of committing depredation thereon contrary to the law of nations, in violation of section sixteen-fifty-one of title eighteen of the United States Code, we the jury find the defendant, James Taylor Clevenger, guilty as charged in the indictment."

Forty seconds, half-a-dozen gavel raps, and the brusque eviction of a woman whispering into a Razr smaller than her COURT TV press tag silenced the post-verdict uproar. While the busted reporter exited, Rep heard Walt Kuchinski's urgent baritone sweep over the courtroom. Kuchinski was only local counsel for Clevenger and his three best suits put together hadn't cost a thousand dollars, but the dream-team superstars brought in from both coasts as lead counsel seemed stunned into paralyzed silence by the verdict.

"Your honor, I ask that the jury be polled by name."

The judge handed a stapled jury list to the clerk, who squared her shoulders as she turned toward the jury. When she spoke, a sharply challenging tone replaced the carefully neutral timbre of her verdict reading.

"Robert Ferguson: Is this your verdict?"

"Yes it is."

"Marilyn Ebelard: Is this your verdict?"

"Yes."

Rep's eyes swiveled to the fifth juror in the first row. He was a twenty-something male with hair the color of old straw. His scared-rabbit eyes blinked through wire-rims too big for his face. He seemed to cringe with each lash-like repetition of the question.

"Elizabeth Pitowski: Is this your verdict?"

"It is."

"Brian Cochrane: Is this your verdict?"

"Yep."

Rep's fingernails bit into his palms as he leaned forward.

"Grady Schoenfeld: Is this your verdict?"

The young man's mouth twisted wordlessly for seven painful seconds.

"Grady Schoenfeld," the clerk barked, "is this—"

"I just don't know!" Schoenfeld pounded a frustrated fist on his thigh. "I said I thought he probably did it, but I'm just *not sure*."

Another eruption. Gavel raps beat a staccato tattoo from the bench. All the lawyers at both tables were now standing and yammering.

"That'll do," the judge said. "Counsel, sit down and shut up. Bailiff, escort Mr. Schoenfeld to my chambers and show the rest of the jurors to the jury room. Everyone else, stand up while the jury goes out, then either sit down or leave—but don't make a peep while you're doing it, or you won't see the inside of this courtroom again."

As he watched the jury file out, Rep sensed his scheduling conference slipping away, along with any chance of a quick, clean end to Angstrom's case. He was wrong. The instant the door closed behind the exiting jurors, the judge crooked his index finger at the *Goettinger v. Angstrom* group, which obediently trooped up to the bench.

"We're gonna be awhile sorting this out. Since my calendar has probably just been blown to hell for the foreseeable future, I have an idea. The newsies are all going to be here waiting for the next thing to happen in this circus or outside reporting on the last thing. The press room should be nice and quiet. As long as you're going to be here for awhile anyway, why don't you go down there and see if you can get this case settled?"

"Your honor," Rep's adversary, Jeff Glendenning said hesitantly, "given the lateness of the hour—"

"Despite the delicate *politesse* of my diction," the judge said, "that was not a suggestion."

They obeyed. Sort of. As they approached the elevators, Glendenning started muttering something. Rep turned toward the burly, white-maned man who towered nearly half-a-foot over Rep's five-nine.

"Gerry and I are going out for some fresh air," he said. "Thirty-thousand for a bullet-proof muzzle, plus we'll drop our claims. Best I can do. Talk it over with your client and we'll see you in twenty minutes."

He didn't wait for an answer. Just walked away and started down the stairs with Geraldine Lindner, Goettinger's in-house general counsel.

"Does he piss you off as much as he does me?" Angstrom asked.

"He's not having a good day," Rep said. "Let's go down and talk."

The judge was kidding about the press room. Milwaukee's federal courthouse doesn't have one. Ordinarily, reporters camp forlornly in the corridors or on the front steps along with everyone else. Rep and Angstrom went to a conference room behind a first-floor bankruptcy court, whose own judge would be busy with insolvencies in Green Bay for a month or so. Given the press attention that the sex-or-swim case had generated, the chief judge had grudgingly allowed the media to base themselves there during the trial instead of cluttering up the rest of the courthouse.

Rep usually enjoyed negotiations, but he couldn't see the point of these. Negotiation is based on information and fear. Rep didn't have enough of the first, and Goettinger Corporation didn't have enough of the second.

"The answer to thirty-thousand is no, by the way," Angstrom said as they worked their way toward the conference room. "But you knew that."

"Best case, you win two-hundred-fifty-thousand on your counterclaim. Worst case, they win their claims and bankrupt you. Lawyers call that an asymmetrical risk. So think hard about your counteroffer."

"What do you recommend?"

"Seventy percent of two-fifty is one-seventy-five." Rep opened the conference room door. "There's no such thing as a seventy percent chance of winning a civil jury trial unless you're in a wheelchair."

"Only twenty-two percent of American adults still smoke," Angstrom said in unruffled disgust as they stepped inside, "and apparently they're all reporters assigned to this case."

"Counteroffer. Focus."

"Well would you look at that? What have we here?"

Rep followed Angstrom's gaze. In the center of the scarred and mottled conference table, surrounded by Styrofoam cups used as ashtrays and evidence of hastily digested pizza, lay a thick, cardboard, aqua-colored file-folder with "**GOETTINGER—RISK MANAGEMENT (2004)**" written on its tab in bold felt-tip.

"An anonymous benefactor, perhaps," Angstrom said.

"No one could have known that we'd be down here alone," Rep said. "If someone planted that folder they weren't leaking it to us. They left it for reporters covering the sex-or-swim case."

"All the better for us then, no?"

Rep gazed at the folder's opaque cover, as if it were a work of art whose deeper meaning would yield to patient study. Angstrom watched him for a few moments, then pulled a chair out and got comfortable, leaning back to balance it on its two rear legs and bracing his forearm against the table's edge.

"You're thinking it's odd that a Goettinger file turns up in the middle of the sex-or-swim case on the day we have a court appearance in a separate case against Goettinger, aren't you?"

"The word 'coincidence' had crossed my mind."

"It's a mystery."

"So is the doctrine of the trinity—or so my wife tells me."

"Well, however it got there, the file is within reach. Perhaps if we page through it the price of poker will go up."

"If we find nothing we will have compromised ourselves to no purpose. If we find something ugly enough to make a difference, on the other hand, we'll have a legal obligation to disclose it. We might make some work for the FBI but because Goettinger would have no reason to pay you to keep it secret, we wouldn't help your case a bit."

"In other words, two things can happen if we look at the file, and both of them are bad."

"Right."

Rep pulled a thick, brown envelope holding a copy of the pleading file out of his saddle-leather briefcase. He stuffed the pleadings themselves back into the briefcase, and then fussed the Goettinger file folder into the envelope. Looking around for a writing instrument more muscular than his blue Bic, he found only a green Magic Marker. He shrugged, sealed the envelope, and then signed his name in garish strokes across the seal.

"Your turn," he said to Angstrom.

"We're not actually going to return this to Goettinger without looking at it, are we?"

"Of course not."

"Then what's this rigamarole all about?"

"We found this on federal property, outside Goettinger's custody and control. We're going to give it to the first deputy marshal we can track down, and tell Goettinger to ask the court if it wants the file back."

"And we're doing this business with the Magic Marker to prove we didn't peek?"

"No. We're doing this to make Goettinger think we did."

Chapter Nine

"No plea bargain," Kuchinski said quietly to Rep as he joined him outside the courtroom some six hours later. "Finnegan won't come off felony."

The two men leaned against the maple railing that surrounded an atrium yawning two stories below them and several more above. Despite the late hour—almost ten—scores of pacing footfalls still echoed off marble floors and walnut wainscoting. The light seemed unnaturally bright in a building that seldom saw much activity after dark.

"Does your jury consultant think the holdout will hang tough?"

"Yep. Same consultant who told us we'd get an acquittal without breathing hard. Ninety-eight thousand dollars for being one-hundred-seventy-nine degrees wrong. Hell, I coulda guessed wrong for ten-thousand."

"Maybe he thought the trial was in California."

"That just might be it. What with global warming and everything, it's an easy mistake to make."

"When did the jury start deliberating again?" Rep glanced at his watch.

"Sevenish. Took the judge quite a while to question them one by one. Then he let them eat dinner while he heard us out on our mistrial motion."

"Three hours and no word. Maybe the consultant is right."

"Miracles happen. Your settlement negotiations have been plugging along since four o'clock or so. It doesn't take that long to say 'no and goodbye.' Is something really happening or are you just trying to make it look good?"

"The other side is polling board members by phone about our latest offer."

"Sounds promising. They wouldn't need the board's permission to settle a case out of petty cash. Why do you look like your client will be writing the check instead of cashing it?"

"Because there's no good reason for them to be talking about that kind of money this early in the game."

"There's always a reason."

"I know," Rep said. "I just said there's no *good* reason."

"Ah. One of those reasons that's a buzz-killer."

Both men turned as they heard steps approaching. Angstrom ambled up to them and rested his hips against the railing.

"Do you two know each other?" Angstrom asked.

"Walt has been kind enough to sub-lease part of his suite in the Germania Building to me while I'm trying to get my firm's Milwaukee office up and running."

"And Rep has been kind enough to dress the place up with framed copies of classic advertising prints and keep the fridge stocked with Leininkugel. Plus he pays the rent on time. That's the real reason I referred you to him. Speaking of which, I wish one of the candy-ass suits he represents would get nailed with a DUI so he could return the favor."

"I'm working on it," Rep said.

"You're a celebrity," Angstrom told Kuchinski then.

"Greta Van Sustern doesn't have me on speed-dial yet."

"The reason I came over," Angstrom said *sotto voce* to Rep, "is that on my way back from the men's room I saw Goettinger's general counsel having a little heart-to-heart with Clevenger's mom. Maybe one more item for the implausible coincidence file."

"Maybe. What do you think, Walt?"

"Not necessarily. Valerie Clevenger did corporate regulatory work for Goettinger even before she turned herself into a white collar crime specialist. Then she handled a criminal investigation that Finnegan was pursuing against the company. They dumped her when Goettinger died a couple of years ago, but she may still know where some bodies are buried."

"Corporate regulatory to white collar crime is kind of a major re-invention," Rep said. "When did she do that?"

"Oh-one, oh-two, something like that. A Houston firm sent her up here to open a Milwaukee office focusing on energy stuff. Hummed along for about ten years, did all the right things, got mentioned in the business press, helped out with the grunt work on the bar committees. But when you have a niche practice and the niche disappears, so does your practice."

"What happened?"

"About five minutes after Enron cratered her partners down in Houston decided they didn't need anyone doing energy work in Milwaukee. Wrote her a check and told her to pursue other opportunities. Instead of finding an inside counsel slot to use as a glide path to retirement, she decided to build herself a white collar crime practice from zero. And damned if she didn't bring it off."

"Even though she'd never been a trial lawyer?"

"Oh, she doesn't do the grubby white collar crimes that go to trial. No doctors triple-billing Medicaid or bartenders keeping two sets of books for her. She does strictly big-league, Fortune Five-Hundred, crime in the suites stuff. Those cases always settle."

"By having the defendant pay a lot of money without admitting that it did anything wrong?"

"Right. Give her credit, though. She got some sweet deals and built a reputation fast. There are some insiders who'll tell you she walked off with Terry Finnegan's testicles in her briefcase more than once."

"Don't look now," Angstrom said, "but Mr. Glendenning is coming our way and looking dyspeptic."

Kuchinski moved discreetly away. Glendenning strode up, his lips slightly parted in an expression that combined resignation and disgust.

"The board won't go one-seventy-five. One-sixty. Half now, half after the first of the year. No interest, no costs, dismissal with prejudice, no book, watertight non-disclosure agreement."

"We've got a deal," Angstrom said before Rep could open his mouth.

"Let's put it on the record," Rep said.

"We might have to wait a bit," Angstrom said. "A gaggle of lawyers just started streaming in."

"Quarrel of lawyers," Glendenning said with considerable asperity. "Gaggle of geese, quarrel of lawyers."

"Whatever it is," Rep said, "let's join them."

They did. The jury box was empty. Eight minutes later, when the judge came in and waved everyone into their seats, it was still empty.

"The jury reports that it's still deadlocked," he said. "I'm going to let them go tonight and come back at nine tomorrow. At *eight* tomorrow you gentlemen will be here, at which time the court will entertain all the motions the defense is panting to make—including, unless I miss my guess, a request that I reconsider my denial of the motion several months ago to dismiss the indictment on its face. Don't draw any inferences about how I might rule if the jury deadlock continues and you guys can't agree on a plea bargain—but one way or another, ladies and gentlemen, we're going to be done with this case by the close of business tomorrow."

The gavel began to fall and Rep began to rise at the same instant.

"Your honor, we have a settlement to report in *Goettinger*."

The gavel didn't stop, but it slowed long enough for the judge to speak one sentence.

"Write it up and send it in." RAP! "I'm glad *someone* in this courtroom knows how to settle a case. Court's adjourned."

The cheerful handshakes that Rep exchanged amid the hubbub in the hallway outside the courtroom came on automatic pilot. He turned his cell-phone on as soon as he legally could in case he had a message from Melissa. Maybe Angstrom's case had ended up morphing into borderline extortion, but he'd save that for a law school exam question in case he ever became a profes-sor. At the moment, Melissa's green-flecked brown eyes, arch banter, and educated sense of the artful massage monopolized his mental processes.

He was finishing one last hand-shake when six bars of *Can-can* announced a call. He almost answered with something sweetly suggestive, then remembered that Melissa might not be the one calling.

She wasn't.

"Mr. Pennyworth?" The voice was female and sounded rather younger than Melissa's thirty-two years. "The attorney?"

Unwilling to tell a bare-faced lie in a federal courthouse, Rep said "Yes."

"My name is Tereska Bleifert. Professor Pennyworth gave me your phone number a couple of weeks ago because I said I might have a question for you, but then I decided not to call you, but now I'm here, and I do want to ask you something, although not the thing I was going to ask in the first place. When she gave me your number. I'm wearing a red sweater and waving my arm."

Rep looked toward the doors to the elevator lobby and spotted her. He'd guessed right about her age. She hadn't seen twenty yet. Fairly recently, from the looks of it, she had shaped her brown hair into a no-nonsense, low maintenance cut that barely reached her neck. As Rep moved toward her, he saw a fiercely intense look in her eyes that tried to seem hard but couldn't quite bring it off. She was standing about three feet from a man whose name Rep didn't know but whom he recognized as a local reporter. The man was edging closer to Bleifert, but Rep didn't pay any attention to that.

"Hi," Bleifert said with a hint of a blush when Rep reached her. "I came down here to pick someone up that I thought would be ready, because the trial was supposed to be over, but I guess it isn't over and I couldn't get into the courtroom and now I can't figure out what's going on."

Rep explained quickly.

"Who were you supposed to pick up?" he asked then, wincing as he imagined Melissa's reaction to ending a sentence with a preposition and disregarding the objective case in the same question.

"One of the jurors. Grady Schoenfeld."

"Uh, yeah," Rep said.

"Is that one *n* or two in 'Pennyworth?'" the reporter asked. "Boone Fletcher, by the way. Two o's."

Chapter Ten

The second Friday in October, 2007

"So Jimmy Clevenger is off the hook?" Melissa asked Rep.

She parked their Taurus behind a brand new, pale green Toyota Prius hybrid about a hundred yards down Terrace Avenue from Villa Terrace, where tonight's Brontë Convocation events would take place.

"Not necessarily off for good. The jury hung and the judge didn't acquit him. He granted a motion to dismiss the indictment on its face. Finnegan plans to appeal, get the ruling reversed, and try again with a different jury."

"Wouldn't that be double jeopardy or something?"

"It's not my field, but Walt says no. Because it was a defense motion and the judge ruled on a question of law rather than fact, Finnegan can get another kick at the cat. All he has to do is convince the Court of Appeals that attempted rape is piracy if you try it on a ship."

"'Yo ho ho and a bottle of rum,'" Melissa said as they climbed out.

"Unless I'm very much mistaken, by the way, that shiny new Prius with the IM4KARL license plate belongs to my recent client. It's the first thing he bought on the strength of the Goettinger settlement."

They strolled together through the comfortable evening air. October weather is fifty-fifty in Wisconsin, and the Brontës had lucked out. When they reached Villa Terrace Rep stopped and frankly gaped.

"Yeah," Melissa said. "The program says we owe this gem to Lloyd R. Smith and his blushing bride—two crazy Milwaukee kids who didn't have a thing in the world except their love for each other and several million dollars."

"And that was back when several million dollars was regarded as a considerable amount of money."

"They went to Italy on their honeymoon and, like every tourist in history except Martin Luther and the odd Visigoth, they fell in love with it. So they decided to bring a little back with them. Several thousand orange barrel tiles, a few tons of Italian limestone, a brace of statues, and *voilá*—their very own Tuscan villa on the east side of Milwaukee."

"Amazing what you can do when there are weak unions and no income taxes."

A large crowd, many in Victorian dress, filled the open-air passageway on either side of the main entrance and clogged the doorway. Rep and Melissa paused about thirty feet away, on the street side of a graceful courtyard. After one look at the crush, Rep suggested skirting around the building to its Lake Michigan side. Melissa quickly agreed.

They had made it more than halfway through haphazard greenery guarding the north side of the building, past a statue of either Hermes or Apollo, when they encountered a mini-copse still sheltered by abundant autumn foliage. At that point a glimpse of buttocks more gently rounded and delicately rendered than any sculptor could have managed startled them.

Not as much, however, as Rep and Melissa startled the owner of the buttocks. She squealed in surprise at the twig-snaps announcing their approach. Leaping nimbly to her feet, she began without undue haste to pull up her jeans. Before Rep and Melissa could afford the lass some privacy by retreating toward the statue, Angstrom rolled out from under the busy young lady and serenely pulled up his zipper.

"Don't forget the blanket," he said gaily to her as he walked away.

He headed toward Rep and Melissa, spritzing his mouth from a tiny bottle of Listerine as he did so. He smiled broadly.

"That Prius is *amazing*. The young lovelies can't talk about anything except 'driving green' and 'reduced carbon footprint.' It's a coed-magnet."

"Well," Rep said as he watched the re-clad damsel make a spirited departure, "at least they're exposing themselves to art."

"I hope you're not *too* shocked." Angstrom fell into step with them on their continued journey toward Villa Terrace's east side. "I make it a point not to roll in the hay with anyone who's taking one of my classes."

"It's nice to have scruples," Melissa said. "I trust your admirer isn't the only UWM student who's coming tonight. The point of having this evening's program here instead of at the Pfister was to raise our visibility a bit by mixing undergraduates with the Brontë enthusiasts."

"Tereska Bleifert made it, along with at least a handful of other students. We should find out around ten o'clock or so whether combining college students and free wine is a good idea."

They rounded the corner, where the vista of a lushly planted garden rolling one-hundred steeply sloping yards toward Lincoln Memorial Drive and Lake Michigan presented itself. Melissa caught her breath.

"Speaking of wine," she said, "I'm definitely in the mood for some."

"Look for Dean Mignon. He is no doubt busily checking the vintages, in case the caterer's selection is too plebian for his standards."

"If that's what he's up to then he must be somewhere in the middle of the patio over there," Rep said, "because it looks like that's where the wine is."

"Happy sipping," Angstrom said. "But don't drink too much before you try the funicular."

Angstrom pointed toward a pulley-operated cab at the south end of the terrace. Big enough for four or five people, it seemed intended for visitors who didn't care to risk Villa Terrace's formidable hill on foot—especially after three or four drinks. Rep noticed Amy Lee, Taylor Gates, and Jimmy and Valerie Clevenger standing beside it.

Melissa tugged Rep toward the patio and a table draped in white linen with stemmed glasses of six different wines lined up in front of their respective bottles. A pinot noir with a rich, almost lustrous color drew her attention. She reached tentatively for a glass.

"Are you a oenophile, professor?"

Recognizing Mignon's voice, she braced herself. She sensed that payback time for her insubordinate defense of 'lesbian rule' was rapidly approaching.

"Not a savvy one. On a good day I can tell cabernet from merlot."

"Please allow me." Mignon offered her an indulgent smile and approached the table like Tiger Woods at Augusta. Hands behind his back, leaning forward in an elegant bow, he carefully examined each row of glasses. He frowned in concentration. Neck muscles tensed under the strain of critical effort. Drawn by the performance, a loose semi-circle of people gathered. Mignon hovered in an agony of delicate judgment over a Bordeaux and a pinot grigio. After seven seconds of delicious suspense he selected the former.

I'm being ribbed, Melissa thought. *I'm supposed to sip the wine, say it's superb, and then blush when he tells me that it's Mogen David vintage last month.* She decided that unless he laid the act on too thick she'd play along.

When Mignon straightened and tendered the sedulously selected vintage to her, she wondered for an instant if she were wrong. His expression seemed so deeply solemn and at the same time so fatuously self-satisfied that she imagined he might actually be serious. When he spoke, though, his words banished all doubt, for he laid the schtick on with a trowel.

"Try this one. It's pert and saucy, with a rich hint of mischief."

Melissa paused for one beat before replying with rather more than a hint of mischief.

"Do you want me to drink it or give it a spanking?"

Titters ran through the crowd. A deep flush suffused Mignon's ample forehead and the tops of his ears. He tried for a game smile, but it flashed weakly on and off, like a light bulb on the verge of burning out.

A spasm of remorse jolted Melissa. *Dear Lord, he WAS serious. I've hurt his feelings for the sake of a one-liner.*

"I appreciate your wit, professor," Mignon stammered, "but I don't think that one should make light of child abuse, even in jest."

Melissa flinched at the sheer silliness of the exaggeration. But Mignon needed a dignified exit, and she wasn't going to deny it to him.

"The intensity of your feelings about child abuse does you a great deal of credit, dean, and you're quite right to remind us about that important issue."

Mignon beamed, unambiguously pleased with himself once again.

"Will you be going inside soon?" he asked.

"In about ten minutes. I need to make sure that the Power Points are properly loaded for the paper I'm supposed to present."

"The hymnals that Professor Angstrom appraised are on display in the Zuber Room. If you get a chance, you might take a look at them."

"I certainly shall."

"Your wife was awesome," Bleifert said to Rep about fifteen minutes later, after Melissa had made her way inside. "Squelching that self-important wine-snob. It was priceless."

"Thank you. I'll pass that on."

"I'm looking forward to the panel. I hope Professor Pennyworth doesn't just read her friend's paper but weighs in on the Q-and-A. That could be very entertaining."

"I wouldn't count on any rhetorical pyrotechnics from Melissa. She enjoys good-spirited verbal jousting with people who can keep up, but she's not a show-off. When she zings someone it's usually in self-defense."

"Right. According to Livy, Rome conquered the world in self-defense."

Bleifert had all of Rep's attention now. A half-smile played at her lips and her eyes glinted with an impertinence that might have gotten her ears boxed in Charlotte Brontë's day. Rep was trying to decide whether the tease was playful or malicious when Bleifert's eyes darted to her left.

"Excuse me, I think I see a chance for a corporal work of mercy. Or maybe a venial sin, but either way I'll feel good about it."

Rep followed her gaze to Valerie Clevenger about eight feet away, gazing with eloquent despair at an open purse and an empty pack of Dunhills. Bleifert took a pack of Marlboro Lights from her purse and flourished it in Clevenger's direction.

"Will these help?"

"You have no idea how much they'll help." The older woman reached out two fingers to fish a cigarette from the pack.

"You'd be doing me a huge favor if you took the whole pack," Bleifert said. "I've decided to quit. Right now. Cold turkey."

"Smart girl. I hope you make it stick." Clevenger put the pack in her own purse after taking a cigarette from it. "If you change your mind, don't be shy about telling me."

She accepted a light that Bleifert offered from a jade-green Bic.

"I won't change my mind. I'm way overdue to stop. It started out as an affectation, turned into a habit, and it's on its way to becoming an addiction."

"Good luck with it. I quit the day after my bar exam and stuck with it for twenty-five years. Then Jimmy was indicted, and look at me now."

"I hope that turns out to be a short-term thing for you," Bleifert said. "I have to run inside now. I'm on the Power Point control board for the panel that starts in twenty minutes, so I have to get in there for a run-through."

"Any word on an appeal?" Rep asked Clevenger as Bleifert strode off.

"They filed the notice of appeal at four o'clock this afternoon. Finnegan must have spent night and day lobbying the Appellate Division in Washington to get authorization this quickly. He also filed a motion for expedited treatment."

"Are you going inside for the panel?"

"I don't think so. Our brief could be due as early as mid-November. I'm going to track down a client who's on the Villa Terrace board, show the flag, and curl up with some case law."

"Happy hunting."

As Rep started toward the door, something on the patio near his feet caught his eye. He stooped to pick it up. It was a gilt-edged picture card, about four inches by two-and-a-half. What kids in Catholic schools used to call holy cards, as Melissa would later explain.

Rep figured it had dropped from Bleifert's purse when she pulled the cigarettes out for Clevenger. It depicted a haloed woman in a caramel colored nun's habit, looking in rapturous ecstasy toward heaven, whence golden light streamed toward her.

Rep turned the card over. Small printing on the back identified the woman as St. Teresa of Avila, but he didn't pay much attention to that. Written down the length of the card in the kind of precise, Palmer Method penmanship that wins gold stars from parochial school teachers were six names. Three of them meant nothing to him, but three others stood out:

René Mignon
Harald Angstrom
Melissa Seton Pennyworth

Chapter Eleven

Subliminal obsession, definitely. Rep glanced surreptitiously at his watch as the paper Melissa was presenting wound toward its studiously understated conclusion. Maybe vituperations against Romanism were common among right-thinking, mid-Victorian, establishment Brits, but the excerpts from Charlotte Brontë's letters that flashed on the screen as Melissa clicked through her Power Points suggested a novelist who spent way more time stewing about stained glass and incense than a sturdy Protestant without her own issues would have.

Just over a hundred people, by Rep's count, offered surprisingly robust applause as Melissa finished. After a polite nod she took her seat next to Gates in a folding chair immediately to the right of the podium.

A woman of matronly age but with the lean and hungry look of a moderator claimed Melissa's place at the rostrum and planted herself there with oaken solidity. Rep groaned inwardly. This would not end soon. Some iron law of literary conferences apparently required that Gates and Mignon comment on the paper Melissa had just read. As neither could be expected to know much about the subject beyond what they'd just heard, they would have to find some way to link the topic to something they did know about.

Gates managed this rather neatly, playing to the audience by comparing Charlotte Brontë with Dan Brown—to the clear advantage of the former. He noted that Brontë at least took responsibility for her opinions instead of putting them in the mouth of a fictional professor who had somehow managed to acquire tenure at Harvard without knowing enough about Renaissance Art to pass a high school AP exam. The Brontëphiles liked that. A lot.

The challenge proved more daunting for Mignon. His intended theme was that popular culture and philosophic truth seldom intersect except by accident. This got him off on the wrong foot, because he had forgotten that Brontë herself was guilty of being popular. As he meandered through the religious explorations of T.S. Eliot, Tennessee Williams, and Madonna, a restless stirring ruffled the room. He affirmed that the Victorians lived in an Age of Doubt where religion was concerned, whereas we live in an Age of Indifference. He waited for the audience to acknowledge the point, while the audience waited for him to make one.

The moderator finally euthanized Mignon's efforts by inviting questions—for any of the panelists, she hastily added. The first went to Gates. So did the second and the third. When Angstrom finally raised his hand with a question for Mignon, the combination of glee and wariness in Mignon's expression struck Rep as almost touching.

"If Charlotte Brontë were writing fiction today, do you think she'd find a way to comment on the controversy over Pope Pius the Twelfth?"

"I would certainly expect a reference or two to major religious leaders who remain silent in the face of epic moral crises," Mignon said.

"That's a bit simplistic, isn't it?" Gates demanded sharply.

Swelling with the confidence of someone back on familiar turf, Mignon seemed to grow three inches in his chair.

"The controversy over the pope's wartime record will doubtless go on for decades. The effects of his actions, for good or ill, could be debated indefinitely. But the fact remains that, whatever he did or didn't do, when Pope Pius the Twelfth faced the greatest moral crisis in the history of the human race, he didn't speak out. Not a word."

This wasn't a laugh line by any stretch of the imagination, but laughter came and Mignon greeted it with a pleased smile. As the laughter grew the smile began a painful morph into puzzlement—a reaction shared by Melissa until she glanced over her shoulder at the Power Point screen.

In fonts so perfectly matching the papers quoted that the excerpts looked like scanned photocopies, in letters enlarged to headline size, she read:

New York Times
March 14, 1940

"Pope is Emphatic about Just Peace: Jews Rights Defended"

New York Times
October 1, 1942

"A study of the words which Pope Pius XII had addressed since his accession…leaves no room for doubt. He condemns the worship of force and its concrete manifestation in the persecution of the Jewish race."

Canadian Jewish Chronicle
September 4, 1942

"Laval Spurns Pope: 25,000 Jews in France Arrested for Deportation"

Gideon Hausner, Israeli Attorney General
Opening Statement—Trial of Adolph Eichman

"…the pope himself intervened personally in support of the Jews of Rome."

It took eight full seconds for Mignon to look reluctantly over his left shoulder, and six more for him to absorb the text. For an eyeblink blind fury contorted the face that he turned back to confront the audience—or, more accurately, to confront Angstrom, for he acted as if everyone else were invisible. Then, after less than a second, he mastered himself. Only a few flecks of white froth clinging pendulously to his lower lip evidenced the rage that Melissa read on his face as it turned.

The moderator prudently reclaimed the floor and pronounced the panel concluded. As Melissa rose and gathered her papers, she caught sight of Angstrom making his way to the back of the room, where Bleifert was shutting down the Power Point equipment. They took a stab at exchanging high fives, and almost got it on the second try.

So they'd set Mignon up. Baited him into a mistake—"not a word," the kind of incautious absolute that academics are trained to avoid—and then slam-dunked him with a handful of in-your-face sound-bites. Melissa frowned. Verbal sparring is supposed to be mental stimulus, not blood sport.

Thinking to offer Mignon some moral support, Melissa turned toward his chair. He was gone. And he had to have left in a very big hurry.

Chapter Twelve

"You're serious?" Rep demanded. "You're going to abandon this gala event full of people dressed like extras in a Merchant/Ivory film and drive to UWM to make sure Mignon isn't about to kill himself?"

"I feel guilty about abandoning you for forty-five minutes, if that helps."

"I can handle that. What I'm having trouble with is the idea that he might slit his wrists over getting one-upped in front of a hundred people at an event no journalist in the country except *maybe* the society reporter for the *Milwaukee Journal-Sentinel* will care about."

"I don't think they've called themselves 'society reporters' since the Ford administration—and you ended that last sentence with a preposition."

"Guilty as charged. Please admire the spunky way I absorbed that rebuke without letting it crush my spirit."

"You have a very healthy ego."

"It's hard to be humble when I'm married to you."

Melissa grinned.

"That's really my point. Mignon is vulnerable in a way that you and I aren't. His career peaked when he got tenure fifteen years ago. He can't get a scholarly paper published to save his life. This incident won't make the papers, but there are plenty of academics here and by Monday morning they'll have Mignon's gaffe flying through cyberspace from one dot.edu to another."

"Scholars in this country apparently don't have enough to do."

"That's the problem. Graduate students hear cautionary tales about squelches like this one. 'Did you know that *sugar* and *sumac* are the only English words beginning with *su* and pronounced as if they began with *shu*?'"

"'Sure.' That's George Bernard Shaw, isn't it."

"Right. Or, 'In English a double-negative is an affirmative and in some languages a double-negative is an enhanced negative, but we know of no language in which a double-affirmative is a negative.'"

"What's the comeback for that one?"

"'Yeah, yeah.'" Melissa smiled. "That actually happened at a philosophy symposium in the 'seventies. It ended a professor's career. I'm worried that Mignon sees himself now as the butt of a story just like that."

"Enough said, on your way." Rep sighed theatrically to underline his self-sacrifice. "I'll pass the time watching Victorian matrons get the vapors."

"Thanks, honey. You're a doll."

"Oh, and if you run into Tereska Bleifert you can return this to her." Rep handed Melissa the holy card. "She seems to have more than a scholarly interest in you and Mignon as well as Angstrom."

Melissa slipped the card into her pocket, pecked Rep's cheek, and hurried away. Rep turned back toward the plunging terrace and the lake vista. He had ribbed Melissa for form's sake, but he actually contemplated the rest of the evening with contented pleasure. True, tedium would define the next hour. (Rep automatically added thirty-three-and-one-third percent to Melissa's temporal estimates.) But the charming tinge of blush pink at the tops of Melissa's ears corroborated the guilt she professed about leaving him in the lurch, which augured well for the post-Villa Terrace part of the evening. He didn't know what penance she had in mind, but he was looking forward to it.

◇◇◇

Melissa flashed her faculty i.d. card at a blinking red dot on a black screen, punched a code into a keypad, and then opened the door at the faculty entrance on Curtin Hall's basement level. On the way over, she had tried Mignon's home, office, and cell-phone numbers without success. More key-card stuff in the elevator, a ride to the eighth floor, and she found herself outside Mignon's office—which was locked and dark. Raps on the door sharp enough to make her knuckles smart produced no response. She put her ear against the door but heard no tell-tale sounds from inside. This was shaping up as a fool's errand.

She thought she heard a foot-shuffle down the hall. Whirling around in hopes of spotting a custodian who might be bluffed into letting her in, she saw nothing. She tried the door again, just for luck. Same result.

I am now officially out of ideas. She called Rep, whose Valentine's present to her four years ago had been a promise to leave his phone off at social occasions, and began speaking after his voice-mail prompt's beep.

"I might be a bit longer than I promised. I want to send Mignon the kind of confidential note you can't just slip it under someone's door. I'm going to email him from my office. I'll get back to you as soon as I can."

She was waiting patiently for the elevator when she heard the scream.

High-pitched and panicky, the shriek had an echoing, metallic ring. Melissa hurried toward the stairwell around the corner from the elevators. It was well after eight o'clock at night, so she had to pull open a massive metal security door to reach the stairs. As she did so, a piercing whistle-screech assailed her ears. UWM gives its coeds police whistles to use in emergencies. Adreneline pumping now, Melissa rushed through the door.

She saw a broad, well-lighted stairway and nothing else. Another shriek sliced through the close, static air, coming from below and bouncing fiercely off unforgiving terrazzo and concrete. Suspecting that she wouldn't be able to reopen the security door from the stair side at this time of night, she took her shoes off and wedged them between the closing door and the center-post. Then, wincing on unprotected feet, she pelted down the stairway.

Nothing on the seventh floor landing. Or the sixth. No more screams or whistles. Fifth floor landing. Nothing.

"What's going on?" Melissa yelled. "Who was screaming?"

She continued going down. The screams had to have come from inside the stairwell. But she reached the bottom without finding a thing. No traumatized victim, no blood, no torn clothing or discarded handbag. She was now facing a basement security door with EMERGENCY EXIT ONLY—ALARM WILL SOUND posted above its zebra-striped latch. Whoever screamed apparently hadn't exited through that door.

Triggering the alarm would presumably get a guard down here fast, but what could she tell him or her? That she'd heard screaming from someone who wasn't there? She didn't feel like adding her name to the unofficial list of hysterical female academics that the campus cops undoubtedly kept.

A bit winded, she climbed back up the stairs. At each landing she checked the door and found it locked. *So how had the screamer gotten out of the stairwell?* She finally made her weary way to the eighth floor.

And stared dumbly at the door. Closed tight. No sign of her shoes.

As a rule, Melissa made an effort to avoid foul language, especially on campus. She did this both as a matter of personal taste and to avoid setting a bad example of verbal laziness for students too prone to it already. This occasion, however, seemed to call for an exception. She cut loose. Not with the usual stream of blasphemies and obscenities available nightly on HBO and Comedy Central. She was, after all, a Ph.D. in English. She began with a couple of ripe selections from Chaucer and then, warming up, plumbed the richest depths of the Anglo-Saxon canon. She included some oaths that Grendel's mom had undoubtedly keened when she got the news about Beowulf, and then threw in a couple of Celtic variations that Boadicea must have screeched while the Romans were flogging her for insolence, just before her rebellion bathed Roman Britain in fire and blood.

Rep, around this time, was at the bottom of the terrace, gazing up at the villa. He could see Gates and Angstrom at the funicular on top of the hill, preparing to climb into the cab. He started to climb back up. In five minutes Melissa would have been gone an hour, and with serene confidence he expected her to appear on the patio at that moment. The funicular, heading down, passed Rep roughly twenty yards on his left when he was just short of halfway up the hill. He had made another five or six laborious strides when yells and oaths behind him seized his attention.

Even in the dark he could see gray mist, not thick enough to be smoke, pouring from the funicular's open door. Gates, sprawled on the terrace after apparently diving from the cab, was scrambling to his feet and hustling back toward the still descending car.

Now about two-thirds of the way down, the funicular jolted to a stop. Rep headed for it. Gates got there first. Covering his nose and mouth with a handkerchief, Gates plunged through the choking mist and began pulling Angstrom from the funicular. Trying to hold his breath, Rep nevertheless caught a lungful of something that smelled like a cross between fertilizer and shoe polish as he reached Gates and Angstrom. His eyes watered without particularly stinging. He grabbed two handfuls of Angstrom's jacket and, fighting against the uncertain footing, pulled with Gates until they had Angstrom clear of the funicular. With the help of a couple of other bystanders, they dragged him another thirty feet, well away from the mist. Angstrom coughed violently, then came to his hands and knees and panted.

"You okay, prof?" Gates asked.

"'An inconvenience is merely an adventure improperly construed.' Chesteron."

Gates favored Rep with one of his lingering and meaningful gazes.

"Sort of puts a new light on that clipping, doesn't it?" he demanded.

◇◇◇

"No, I will not wait here," Melissa said patiently (for her) to the guard at Curtin Hall's main security desk. The alarm she had triggered by going through the basement security door was still clanging, so she had to raise her voice. "My shoes are missing, my stockings are ruined, and my feet are bruised. If campus security wants me, I'll be in my office."

"But there may still be an intruder in the building."

"That's possible, but I think—" The clanging suddenly stopped, and Melissa found herself shouting at someone two feet away. She lowered her voice. "But I think the chances of him hanging around after all this racket are pretty slim, whereas my chances of having feet that are cold and sore unless I get some shoes on are one-hundred percent."

"At least let me go with you."

Seeing no way she could decently refuse, Melissa adopted what Rep called her nun-drawing-to-an-inside-straight expression and demurred. She didn't think an intruder had assaulted anyone in the stairwell. She thought something else was going on, and she had a pretty good idea of what it was. For the moment, though, she didn't plan on sharing it with anyone except Rep.

After an elevator ride to the second floor, she and the guard began the familiar trek down the central corridor toward her office. As they were hiking through the History Department, she noticed bright light spilling into an intersecting hallway.

"I think that's Professor Angstrom's office," she said.

"Must be working late."

"I saw him at Villa Terrace about an hour ago, and he wasn't acting like someone who was planning on burning any midnight oil."

They turned toward the light. Well before they got there, the guard pushed in front of her and put his hand on a canister of Mace on his belt. He reached the door a few seconds before Melissa's smarting feet could get her there and squatted to examine the lock.

"Tool marks." He pointed to long, angry scratches on the bolt and ugly gouges on the wood inside the face-plate.

Melissa pushed open the door and saw a thoroughly ransacked office. An obstacle course of scattered paper, flung books, and emptied files littered the floor from the doorway to the Power Point projector flush with the front of the desk. The drawers on the file cabinets hung open.

Amidst all this professorial flotsam and jetsam, one item leaped out. In the center of Angstrom's desk, atop a mound of open books, lay a manila folder. Written in bold, felt-tip characters across its front was **Pius XII**. It was empty.

Chapter Thirteen

The cops got to Villa Terrace eight minutes after Rep and Gates pulled Angstrom from the funicular. Boone Fletcher's chocolate brown Honda Civic screeched to a stop eight feet beyond the squad car sixty seconds later. He loped toward Rep and Gates with what looked like a Dictaphone on steroids in his left hand, shoulder-length hair flying behind him as if it were still 1969. Cargo pants flapped loosely around his legs. His cardinal red sweatshirt depicted Bucky Badger, the University of Wisconsin-Madison mascot, in the apparent act of sodomizing a University of Minnesota Golden Gopher.

"The egghead just get drunk, or what?" he asked by way of introduction. "And what's the deal with the smoke they were yapping about?"

"He's not drunk," Gates said. "He was perfectly sober when he got into the funicular with me. By the way, I'm—"

"Famous writer, I know. Guns, girls, and gelignite. Got it. Now what was the smoke all about?"

"We were halfway down the hill when this gray canister sailed into the cab through the window on the far side, spewing mist. Mist, not smoke."

"Any idea what the mist was?"

"No, except it was thick and unpleasant."

"More like Extacy or more like crystal meth?"

"I wouldn't know," Gates said coldly.

"I know, I'm just goofing on you." Fletcher stepped back and took a more searching look at the funicular. "Kind of a funny place for a gas attack. Windows on three sides, slow moving, easy to escape."

"It didn't happen the way I'd write it in one of my stories."

"Describe the canister."

"About the size of a small bottle of Diet Coke. Sounded like metal when it hit the floor. It's probably still in there."

Fletcher gave Gates two raised eyebrows and a quick point with his index finger while he mouthed a slow and exaggerated, "Good point." He had taken two steps toward the funicular when a voice barking behind him stopped the third step with his foot still six inches off the ground.

"Contaminate that crime scene, scribbler, and I'll kick your butt from here to Walker's Point."

"Why, Stan," Fletcher said, whirling around and spreading his arms in a theatrically welcoming gesture. "Sergeant Stanley Mittlestedt, everybody. Twenty-some years on the force and a service jacket cleaner than my permanent record at Saint Roberts grade school."

As Fletcher strolled toward the policeman, Rep looked at his watch and frowned. He frowned through the message Melissa had left, and was still frowning four cell-phone rings later when he got her voice-mail prompt. He left a message more worried than it would have been twenty minutes before.

He had missed her by less than a minute. After thanking the earnest young campus cop for escorting her to her office, Melissa settled at her desk and pulled out her keyboard, in ostensible preparation for an indefinite period of work. She smiled at the cop's appraising gaze as he lingered in the doorway, then waved to him. He finally took the hint and left.

Her email to Mignon took two minutes. She waited four more to give the cop time to make tracks. On the elevator back to the eighth floor, she switched her cell-phone to vibrate. She figured Rep might be calling, and she didn't want a ring to give her away while she was lurking near Mignon's office.

Forty feet of dark hallway still separated her from the office when her phone's gyrations signaled Rep's call. She retreated into the shadows, debating whether to answer long enough to whisper that she'd call back in ten minutes.

She was reaching for the phone when she sensed movement in the darkness at the end of the corridor. She froze. Rep would have to wait. Fortunately, eight years of marriage had given him plenty of practice. She peered fiercely into the blackness, wondering if she'd actually seen or heard anything at all.

A quicksilver splash of light answered the question. Two seconds worth of brightness burst out of the stairwell as the security door opened. She saw someone dart through the doorway. It looked like a woman, but she wouldn't have given better than two-to-one odds on that.

No point in running after whoever it was. With a head start of at least twenty-five seconds, the fugitive could easily reach the exit before Melissa got a glimpse of her or him. She caught her breath, let her pulse rate drift back toward two digits, and resumed her trek toward Mignon's office.

She once again found the door tightly locked. Squatting, she peered at the area around the knob in the faint light from her cell-phone's screen, looking for scratches and gouges like those she seen at Angstrom's office.

The bolt snapped and door opened. She managed to stand all the way up by the time Mignon said, "Good evening, professor."

"Good evening, dean." Her words sounded sheepish to her. She felt a bit like she'd been caught trying to sneak a Coors into the junior prom.

"I received your email a few minutes ago. Thank you for your kind words and your offer of support on the document front."

He enunciated the words with the elaborate precision of someone not altogether sure of his tongue, and she could smell something a lot stronger than merlot on his breath.

"I'll be happy to do what I can. Unfortunately, it looks like the document may have been pilfered from Professor Angstrom's office."

"How very odd. Perhaps we should defer further discussion until Monday. I'm a bit tired right now."

"Of course. The reason I came by, though, was to see whether the same person who broke into Professor Angstrom's office also burgled yours."

"I don't think so. I expect I would have noticed."

I don't think so either. Melissa glanced unconsciously at the lock-plate. *But someone tried.*

Roughly forty-five minutes after they'd gotten back to their condo, by Rep's estimate, Melissa rested her wrists on his shoulders and with infinite finesse began to scratch the top of his back with her fingernails. The gentle stimulus sent waves of contentment coursing through him.

Geisha and client? Rep willed himself to relax, letting his knees sink into the seven-knot Oriental rug on their living room floor.

"Reppert, dearest?"

Definitely not geisha and client.

"Yes, beloved?"

"I have a question about privilege."

Strict attorney and fibbing witness? Haven't done that one in a while.

"I'm good at privilege. Ask away."

"If I tell you something about this Angstrom mess tonight that I didn't tell the police, would it be all right for you to keep it just between us, or would that make you a naughty lawyer?"

"Absolutely privileged. In the eyes of the law, you and I are a single entity. 'Two souls in one body,' as the older cases put it."

"That's kind of sweet," Melissa sighed. "Almost poetic."

"Well, the same poets who came up with that used to hang twelve-year olds for stealing six shillings, so let's get to the prosaic part of this problem."

"Oh dear. Mood killer?"

"No, this mood is a survivor. But for the moment let's focus on whatever is bothering you."

"Correct as usual, King Friday. Get our robes and I'll put coffee on."

Rep managed his part of the assignment, tripping only twice on shoes and clothing strewn over the carpet. In minutes they were demurely draped in flannel robes, holding steaming cups of coffee, and two sentences into an all-business conversation.

"Okay," Rep said, beginning sentence-three, "why didn't you tell the police that Bleifert was the one who tried to break into Mignon's office?"

"I said 'might well have been the one.'"

"Who's the lawyer here? I'll handle the pettifogging."

"I'm not nit-picking. I saw the Power Point equipment in Angstrom's office. The most logical explanation is that Bleifert returned it, which probably means she had a key that he gave her for the purpose."

"If she had a key for that office she wouldn't have broken into it."

"Precisely." Melissa sipped coffee, then blew across the top of her cup.

"We may have a second entrant, who also tried the Mignon break-in. Or my premise is wrong and she wasn't the one who returned the Power Point equipment and is therefore possibly responsible for both the actual break-in and the attempted one."

"Fine. It could have been Bleifert who lured you into the stairwell so she could try her luck with Mignon's office, or it could have been someone else. The evidence is inconclusive. Sounds like a dandy little job for the police."

Melissa hesitated. She didn't confuse feeling with thinking. She felt a warm glow for her alma mater, the University of Michigan, but that had nothing to do with how she filled out her NCAA brackets each March.

"I think Tereska Bleifert is psychologically fragile. Smart as a whip and studious, but about as worldly as a novice in a 1950s convent. She's out of the south-side home/church/school cocoon for the first time in her life. She's either a very spiritual person, or she's neurotically obsessed with Catholicism."

"Or both."

"Or both." Melissa nodded.

"And if she's on the edge of a nervous breakdown, you don't want to be the one who pushes her over."

"That makes it sound like I'm thinking with my heart."

"No, you're thinking with your gut. There's a difference. For someone with sound instincts, like you, it makes sense. Please note that I said 'sense' and not 'sensibility.'"

"You are *asking* for it, mister." Melissa giggled, relaxing as she realized that Rep understood. "But that's the bottom line. Speculative suspicion isn't enough for me to sic cops on an emotionally at-risk innocent."

"Which speaks well of you. But that charming ingénue wrote six names on the back of a card, and within the space of half-an-hour tonight three of them were the object of physical attack, burglary, or false imprisonment. One of those names was yours, and I don't like the odds."

"I think I can explain the card. During Lent pious Catholics pray for Catholics who can't receive communion during the Easter season because they're in a state of mortal sin. I'm in that category, in her eyes, because I'm an apostate. Mignon probably is too. The names are in different colored ink, suggesting that she wrote them down at different times. I'm betting that she added my name after I casually mentioned that I was a convent school girl who was now agnostic."

"I'm officially blown away," Rep said after taking a moment to digest the data-dump and parse Melissa's logic. "You get credit for the fastest segue from heart to head since Elinor Dashwood in *Sense and Sensibility*."

"Who's the professor here? I'll handle the pretentious literary allusions."

"But wouldn't she have to have kind of a long list? The way she sees it, isn't everyone who's not a practicing Catholic in a state of mortal sin?"

"No, dear, that's a heresy. The Church's theory is that a benighted Protestant like you hasn't had a fair shot at eternal truth yet. You can save your soul just by showing through a good life that you're open to God's grace, even though your invincible ignorance keeps you from embracing His Church."

"Whereas you can't plead ignorance as a defense?"

"Right. I had my chance and turned my back on it. So unless I repent, then as Tereska sees things I'm in for a rather warm time of it."

"It seems kind of unfair," Rep mused. "Have you thought of taking a stab at repenting, just to hedge your bets?"

"Theologians call that 'Pascal's Wager.' Even if the odds against the Church being right are a million to one, a one-in-a-million risk of becoming the main course in an eternal barbecue argues for going to mass."

"But you're betting the other way."

"The only God I could believe in would punish intellectual dishonesty far more harshly than apostasy. Anyway, to circle back to Tereska, hypothesizing a touching concern for my immortal soul makes more sense than believing she goes around throwing canisters of gas at people."

"You know her better than I do."

"So. Should I give her up to the police?"

Rep thought for about thirty seconds. He picked invisible specks of lint from his robe between two sips of coffee. Then he spoke.

"No. We have nothing to tie her to the gas attack, and for all we know the stuff at UWM was just academic shenanigans—a glorified panty raid. We'll do our job and let the cops do theirs. Agreed?"

"Agreed. As the frisky medieval maiden said to the pedo-philiac prince, 'We're on the same page.'"

"That's a mood enhancer."

"It was intended to be."

PART TWO
It's Funny Until Someone Gets Hurt

"It's funny until someone gets hurt."

—Mom

Chapter Fourteen

The third Monday in October, 2007

T. S. Eliot was dead and Caucasian, so the man with East Asian features approaching Melissa's classroom just before three p.m. was most likely someone else. Which was too bad, because a non-poet dressed in a three-piece, pin-striped, navy blue suit would probably be bringing unwelcome news—especially if he was the non-poet who had played phone-tag with her all morning in an unsuccessful effort to schedule a meeting.

He was.

"Good afternoon, Professor Pennyworth. "I'm Robert Y. Li."

Melissa flirted with a joke about how *He's a Rebel* would sound in Mandarin, but decided to skip it. This was a good move.

"I've heard it," Li said, reading her mind. "I've heard them all. I'm general counsel for the university. We've been missing each other."

"I'm delighted to meet you, Mr. Li, but I'm teaching a class on the nineteenth century English novel in less than two minutes."

"Standard apologies *et cetera*, but I'm hoping you might trust today's class to your TA. Carolyn Hoeckstra found my inability to extract a mutually convenient meeting time from you and Ms. Bleifert frustrating. She isn't accustomed to frustration and she is therefore now camped in my office."

"Teaching assistants don't do plagiarism checks on term-papers for junior faculty, much less teach classes. I don't suppose she could spend sixty minutes on a campus tour, could she?"

"Patience is not her outstanding virtue. If you could come up with some way to accommodate her I would be very grateful—and the gratitude of lawyers is a commodity even rarer than the time of teaching assistants."

Well, that's clear enough, isn't it?

"Give me thirty seconds."

She entered the classroom, stepped in front of the desk, and looked out over the aggressively unimpressed faces of forty-two students. At least half of them were there solely to check off a core-curriculum requirement without tackling poetry or Middle English.

"The syllabus didn't promise in-class writing exercises, so this is a bonus. No extra charge. Proposition: Austen wasn't the last of the classicists, she was the first of the romantics. Reject or defend. Forty minutes. Go."

She executed a parade ground left face and strode toward the door. She ignored the mutterings of "bitch" that followed her, figuring that they were fair enough. When she heard a single, hissed "bastard" she looked over her shoulder only long enough to say, "Let's leave my parents out of it."

"Commendably old school," Li said as they began walking briskly down the corridor. "Well done."

"If you let diction slide, especially in obloquy, you might as well be teaching business administration."

"How did you miss becoming a lawyer?"

"I married one."

"That would explain it."

"I take it Ms. Hoeckstra is used to getting her own way."

"Her father was Timothy Goettinger, grandson of Wilhelm Goettinger, who founded Goettinger Corporation. She has an office in the Wilhelm Goettinger Wing of the Mechanical Studies Building at the Milwaukee School of Engineering, where she administers the Wilhelm Goettinger Memorial Educational Trust. UWM likes to maximize opportunities for its own engineering graduates, and therefore finds it useful to maintain a strong working relationship with the buzz-cuts at MSOE—especially the buzz-cuts sitting on top of scads of money."

"Where does Ms. Hoeckstra stand on purloined papal documents?"

"I don't think she cares about them. Her concern is Goettinger Corporation, whose history Professor Angstrom was writing."

"Leading to unpleasant litigation in which my husband represented Professor Angstrom. I hope she doesn't think I have any inside information about that—or that I could share it with her if I did."

"I doubt that very much. Whoever broke into Angstrom's office was presumably after something. I suspect that she wants to know whether that something related to Goettinger and, if so, what it was and where it is."

They left Curtin Hall and angled toward a brick and glass tower where the university found office space for non-academic administrators.

"You have my report on Saturday's incident and I assume you have Ms. Bleifert's as well."

"People don't always put everything they know in reports," Li said. "I suspect she's hoping a little heart-to-heart might draw you out a bit more."

Carolyn Hoeckstra was the second thing Melissa noticed when she stepped into Li's office eighty seconds later. The first was the largest telescope she had ever seen outside an observatory. It rested on a chest-high, cherry wood tripod next to a tall south window, dwarfing the green-bound legal tomes that lined the shelves of the intersecting wall.

Hoeckstra sat with crossed legs in front of Li's desk. She seemed dressed for church on Easter Sunday, in a pearl gray silk jacket-and-skirt suit, ivory satin blouse, ecru stockings, and black heels. She wore them like a costume, the kind of outfit someone who spends most of her time in jeans and pullovers throws on three times a year for special occasions. Her blond hair was styled in a brisk, no-nonsense flip that would be good to go seven or eight brush strokes after she got out of bed.

She didn't look like she'd hit thirty yet, but something about her beyond the retro-*Vogue* outfit seemed distinctly un-young, almost consciously anachronistic. Her wristwatch, Melissa realized, that was it. No more than ten percent of Melissa's students bothered with them. Most just checked their cell-phones if they wanted the time. Hoeckstra had burdened her wrist with what looked like two-thousand dollars worth of oversized chronometry, complete with movable, beaded bevel, four function buttons, and enough inset mini-dials to tell time from Tashkent to Toledo—the one in Spain *or* the one in Ohio.

Heirloom from dad. Has to be.

Li introduced Hoeckstra to Melissa, then picked up his phone and instructed someone to "show Ms. Bleifert in." Bleifert promptly appeared. Hoeckstra started talking about five seconds after that, while Bleifert was still looking for a place to sit.

"I apologize for this imposition," she said in a clipped, attention-to-orders voice. "I won't take up any more of your time than necessary."

"What can we do for you?" Li asked.

"I have the following information. One: some material was stolen from Professor Angstrom's office last Friday. Two: Ms. Bleifert was the first one to see the office after the break-in. And three: Professor Pennyworth was with the campus cop who came upon it shortly afterward."

"No argument so far," Li said.

"I told the campus police what I know," Bleifert said. "I have a copy of the report they prepared. You're welcome to take it, if you like."

"I already have one. It's quite clear, as was Professor Pennyworth's."

"In that case," Melissa said, "why are having this conversation?"

Hoeckstra pulled a mini-legal pad from purse.

"I paid a lawyer three-hundred dollars an hour to write this, so I want to be sure I get it right: 'If anyone provides me with information leading to recovery and return to me of all copies of documentary information in any form relating to Goettinger Corporation that was taken from Professor Angstrom's office Saturday night, I will pay a reward of ten-thousand dollars in money or money's worth, as is, where is, without warranty or representation of provenance, no questions asked.'"

"What?" Li asked.

"You paid three-hundred dollars an hour for *that*?" Melissa asked.

"Are you inferring that I'm a thief?" Bleifert asked.

"Certainly not," Melissa said. "She's *implying* that you're a thief. And she's not exactly nominating me for Citizen of the Year, either."

"Now, now," Li said, "don't blame the client for her attorney's tactlessness."

"I didn't mean to insult anyone," Hoeckstra said. "Useful knowledge isn't *necessarily* guilty knowledge."

Necessarily? Melissa saw Bleifert begin fumbling with her purse, and surmised that she had picked up Hoeckstra's stress on the adverb as clearly as Melissa herself had.

"If you're looking for a cigarette, could you skip it for ten more minutes?" Hoeckstra asked. "I hate to sound prissy, but it really does annoy me."

"I don't have any anyway," Bleifert said. "I gave my last pack away on Friday when I impulsively decided to quit smoking."

"Thank you," Hoeckstra said. "Now, if I've offended you—"

"*If* you've offended me?" Bleifert erupted. "If I'd grown up on the east side instead of the south side and my mother was a lawyer instead of a keypuncher, would you be offering me money to tell the truth or not keep something that didn't belong to me?"

"Well, yeah, actually. Although I guess I'd be offering more."

"Go to hell."

"Save the class warfare number," Hoeckstra said as she stood up. "I've heard it all before. I've worked at least as hard in my life as you have. I know what it's like to scrape industrial lubricant out from under your fingernails at the end of a shift."

"You don't know what it's like to know you'll be scraping it out every working day of your life for forty years."

"Have it your way," Hoeckstra sighed. "I'm a class enemy. Fine. Lenin would have had me shot. But Lenin is dead and I'm alive and my offer is on the table. We can do it the hard way or the easy way. Your call. Three-five-one-one-seven-zero-seven. Think it over."

Melissa deliberately waited until Hoeckstra was halfway out the door before she called out, "That was three-five-one-one-seven-oh-seven?"

Hoeckstra half-turned with an ambiguous look on her face, as if not sure whether she was being teased.

"Seventeen-*zero*-seven. 'Oh' is a letter. The number is zero."

Then she left.

"Well, *that* could have gone better," Li said.

"It wasn't your fault," Bleifert told him.

"Neither was the My Lai massacre, but I still feel bad about it."

"What was that hard-way-or-easy-way stuff? Do I need a lawyer?"

"When someone asks if they need a lawyer, the answer is generally yes."

"So that would be you, then?"

"I'm the university's lawyer."

"Cardinal Newman defined a university as a community of scholars."

"The State of Wisconsin defines this particular university as a body corporate *sui juris*, and since Wisconsin pays the bills around here I'm afraid its opinion carries more weight than Cardinal Newman's."

"I'll check with Rep, if you like," Melissa said.

"No, you know what?" Bleifert snapped. "Skip it. This was a set-up."

"No," Li said, "it was a screw-up. Mine. But if incompetence were malice, *Time* magazine would lose a lot of libel suits."

"What's that in plain English?"

"If I'd had any idea she was going to pull that I wouldn't have let her confront you without preparation. I was expecting a heartfelt plea for helpful information, not Catherine de Medicis on steroids."

"*What* information?" Bleifert demanded with fierce intensity.

"Yes, that is the question, isn't it?" Li commented.

"Did Professor Angstrom ask you to do anything in connection with his history of Goettinger Corporation?" Melissa asked.

"No."

"He'd better not have," Li said. "Faculty can freelance if they want to, but they can't use university resources for their private projects. He shouldn't even use his office phone for that stuff, much less a student aide."

"All right." Bleifert let out an exasperated exhalation that charmingly fluttered wisps of hair straying over her forehead. "I learned nothing about Goettinger from Professor Angstrom. I took nothing from his office. I don't know what anybody else took from his office. Clear?"

"Pellucid," Li said. "And you didn't even have to pay someone three-hundred dollars an hour to write it for you."

"That's a pretty good line," Bleifert said as she stalked toward the door, "but I'm not in a mood to appreciate it. See ya."

"Exit Bleifert," Melissa said.

"Carolyn Hoeckstra isn't a bad person," Li said. "But she's a quant, not a creative, as those business administration types you despise would put it. Her strength is numbers. She buys the words, and the words she bought for today created the wrong impression."

"If I'd had you hearing my confessions when I was twelve I'd never have gotten any penance." Melissa rose and prepared to go.

"Just give her the benefit of the doubt. And you might note that Ms. Bleifert did *not* say that she didn't have any information about Goettinger Corporation. She just said she hadn't gotten any from Angstrom."

Already at the door, Melissa paused and thought for a moment.

"You're absolutely right."

Chapter Fifteen

The third Friday in October, 2007

"If you walked into a place called The Twisted Fork in San Francisco," Rep commented, "you'd expect busboys in leather aprons and waitstaff with handcuffs. In Milwaukee, it's just an upscale restaurant."

"I don't know about that," Melissa said. "In San Francisco, arugula this good would probably qualify as a sexual experience."

"Like most sexual experiences," Kuchinski said, "I can't spell it. The government filed its brief in the sex-or-swim case late this afternoon, by the way. More than a month early. The legal writing equivalent of the speed of light. Mr. Finnegan wants that appeal heard in a big damn hurry."

"Any idea why?" Melissa asked.

"You may find out tonight if you accept Boone Fletcher's invitation to track him down at Major Goolsby's later on. He knows almost everything, and what he doesn't know he makes up."

"How did the government's brief look?" Rep asked.

"Scared the hell out of *me*, but the dream-teamers will take it in stride."

"Those guys don't impress you too much, do they?" Melissa asked.

"I'm not wild about having a case jerked out from under me and handed to a couple of celebrity lawyers. When you're picking a jury for a rape case with your nose stuck so far in a jury-consultant's report that you don't notice one of the prospective jurors is wearing a Take Back the Night button, you're not likely to impress me much."

"That raises an interesting point," Rep said. "The last time I hired a jury consulting service it charged my client eighty-thousand dollars, and that was for barebones work without any frills at all."

"This one had plenty of frills. They pulled out all the stops to get a good cross-section on that mock-jury panel. That's how I ran into your buddy Angstrom. They used him to round up some part-time students to flesh out the demographic. And he didn't come cheap, either."

"So Valerie Clevenger not only paid for that, she brought in two left-coast celebrity lawyers. She has to have shelled out, let's see, carry the two, something north of four-hundred-thousand dollars in litigation costs."

"No comment," Kuchinski said.

"White collar crime work must pay better than I thought."

"Any idea why Fletcher wants to talk to Rep?" Melissa asked.

"Well, he has been on the sex-or-swim case since before it was a case."

"You might say he was immersed in it from the beginning," Rep said.

"I'd work up some comeback about that comment being all wet, but we'll save that for the movie version. Point is, that boy thinks he's on to something big. Just ask him."

"Something big?" Fletcher bellowed ninety-five minutes later in the non-smoking section of Major Goolsby's bar and grill. "I'll tell you about big. If all I get for this is the Pulitzer Prize I might not even show up for the ceremony. Anything short of a Nobel and I'll be sulking."

"We're used to that," a man wearing a 1982-vintage Brewers uniform jerseywith Robin Yount's name and number on it said.

"This gentleman, by the way, is Quintus Ultimusque Kazmaryck," Fletcher said.

"'Fifth and Last,'" Rep translated, with a hint of puzzlement in his voice.

"Whoa, how'd you do that?" Fletcher demanded. "You're way too young to have learned Latin as an altar boy."

"Law school. Picked up just enough Latin to mispronounce *prima facie*."

"Q had four siblings, you see," Fletcher said.

"Stop it," Kazmaryck said.

"The youngest was seven when Q's mom missed her period because of him. His dad wanted to leave no doubt that Q would be the end of the line."

"So I ended up with a Catholic joke for a name," Kazmaryck said.

"If your parents had been atheists you might have ended up in the bottom of a d-and-c pail," Fletcher said.

"True. It gives me an excuse for being risk averse."

"Appearances to the contrary notwithstanding," Fletcher said as he took a hit from a schooner of beer, "that was background, not digression. I want you to help me get this story."

"What makes you think I can help?" Rep asked.

"What makes you think I'm talking to you, counselor?" Fletcher paused for a beat, then grinned. "Gotcha. After that lame gas attack at Villa Terrace, I could tell you were worried about Frauen Professor Pennyworth still being at UWM, where it happens Angstrom's office was broken into. I figured she might be up to her Phi Beta Kappa key in this, and your eyebrows almost touching your scalp just now tells me I might be onto something."

"'More matter, less art,' to coin a phrase," Melissa said, as her knee ungently nudged Rep's in a spousal admonition not to react.

"Fair enough, Lady MacBeth."

"Technically, that was Queen Gertrude, from *Hamlet*."

"My bad. Anyway, start with the last night of the sex-or-swim trial. Grady Schoenfeld is the only juror who didn't think Clevenger was guilty, and not long after that Schoenfeld's main squeeze shows up in court looking for Reppert. Plus, Reppert—I can call you Reppert, can't I?"

"I've been called worse, by better men than you."

"Burn," Kazmaryck said, with the lip-smacking delight of a connoisseur.

"Anyway, plus Reppert is office-mates with Milwaukee's very own Perry Mason, the gruff-but-lovable shyster who just happens to be representing Jimmy Clevenger."

"I'm keeping up so far," Melissa said. "So what?"

"No idea. I mean not the foggiest notion. I'm a simple, Midwestern police-beat reporter, and I couldn't connect the dots on something this ungodly complicated if my next Baggie of Vancouver Premium Blend cannabis sativa depended on it. That's why I want your help."

"It's nice to be wanted," Rep said, paying Melissa back for her knee-nudge as her mouth opened and closed.

"Why should you help me? Funny you should ask."

"Because anonymous sources end up looking better in investigative journalism pieces than their subjects do," Rep said.

"Son of a *bitch*," Kazmaryck said. "He saw right through you."

"Get to work on your beer, Q. If we don't kill this pitcher by closing time, the terrorists win. And even without you I am overmatched tonight."

"Not a new experience for you."

"Well, you got me there. You're right, Reppert. Reason number one is that when you give me information you get to spin me."

"You mean there's another reason?"

"Well, there's *quid pro quo*. I'm a fair guy. I get information, I give information. Why would a couple of innocent bystanders like you care about information from the likes of me? Just because Reppert shares an office with Kuchinski, who'd like to be the local hero in a big case?"

"Something to keep in mind," Rep said.

"Close the sale, you dumb mick," Kazmaryck said.

"A taste," Fletcher said, holding up an admonitory finger. "A flash of what's under the pasty, to mix metaphors."

"That is *not* a mixed metaphor, by the way," Kazmaryck said. "That is at most a meta-three, and maybe only a meta-two."

"You see," Fletcher said, "Q here doesn't just run a locksmith and collectibles shop where all goods and services are sold for cash only."

"No credit," Kazmaryck said. "Don't believe in it."

"He's also a politician. And a good one. He's never won an election."

"Zero for thirteen," Kazmaryck said happily.

"In its passion for clean government, the State of Wisconsin provides public financing for legislative campaigns."

"God bless Fighting Bob LaFollette."

"Of course, any campaign needs a good campaign manager."

"I'm a very good campaign manager," Kazmaryck said. "And I work cheap. I don't charge an arm and a leg like those sharks from out of town."

"Plus space for campaign headquarters."

"Plenty of room in my shop, and the rent is very reasonable."

"And then there are campaign posters and brochures."

"Amazing what they charge for those things."

"Although, remarkably enough, the union shops that supply such ephemera seem to require a lot of locksmith work in years divisible by two."

"Always buy union, that's my motto," Kazmaryck said. "Solidarity forever. The union makes us strong."

"Bottom line," Fletcher said, "Q is plugged in."

"That was quite a segue," Rep said.

"Entertaining, though," Melissa said.

"We aim to please. Give our friends some inside dope, Q."

"Assistant United States Attorney Terence Finnegan would very much like to be Attorney General of the State of Wisconsin," Kazmaryck said.

"And who can blame him? The last Democrat who could get through the day without a beer and served as attorney general is now governor. Once you're a governor you start humming *Hail to the Chief* in the shower."

"He has nurtured this hope for at least five years," Kazmaryck said. "He has gotten convictions or headline-worthy settlements in many cases that warm progressive hearts."

"A suit on a perp-walk gladdens the liberal soul," Fletcher said.

"A number of other Democrats, however, would also like to be attorney general, some of whom do not suffer from the handicap of being male."

"That's a pretty serious insinuation," Rep said.

"What, that Finnegan is a male? I can back it up."

"No, that Finnegan bootstrapped a low-rent sexual assault charge into a federal crime so that he could buff up his credentials with feminist activists."

"Did I say that?" Kazmaryck asked Fletcher.

"Libel lawyers call it 'colloquium,'" Fletcher said. "Comes up all the time in the newspaper business—especially the stories I work on, for some reason. Don't sweat, though. It's probably covered by your homeowner's policy—right, counselor?"

"I'm just a copyright lawyer," Rep said, hiding an internal wince.

"Right, I forgot that for a minute. Anyway, got anything for me?"

"A business card with a cell-phone number on it that I only give to my very best clients," Rep said as he and Melissa got up and began to move away from the table. "I'll see if I can come up with anything more substantial."

"That would be appreciated," Fletcher said, looking thoughtfully upward and raising his beer schooner. "And don't bother with the stuff about how that so-called gas canister at Villa Terrace was just a can of wasp-spray painted gray, with the top twisted off with pliers. Sergeant Mittlestedt figured that out before the evidence techs got there."

Rep stopped and looked back.

"I wouldn't want to be in Taylor Gates' shoes," he said.

"Neither would I," Fletcher commented, without turning his head toward Rep. "Like you said, it's better to be a source than a subject."

Chapter Sixteen

The second Friday in December, 2007

Rep still hadn't come up with anything for Fletcher two months later, when the United States Court of Appeals for the Seventh Circuit heard oral argument in the sex-or-swim appeal. That didn't reflect sloth on Rep's part but a rocket docket in Chicago. The court had scheduled argument with unwonted celerity.

"When criminals lose appeals here," Melissa whispered to Rep as they settled into the eighteenth floor courtroom, "do they go to prison or does the floor just open up and drop them straight into hell?"

"The ambience is formidable," Rep agreed.

A ripple of excitement stirred the spectators as the lawyers in the case ahead of *United States v. Clevenger* packed up their papers and prepared to leave. Appellate court audiences are usually just the lawyers paid to be there. Not today. In addition to Rep and Melissa, the crowd included Valerie Clevenger and Carolyn Hoeckstra; Boone Fletcher and at least two other reporters that Kuchinski had pointed out; a crowd of activists whose views could readily be surmised even though they'd had to leave their Say-No-to-Rape pins at the metal detector downstairs; and Quintus Ultimusque Kazmaryck, sitting next to another politico younger and glossier than he.

Augmenting this array at the last minute was René Mignon, who came just in time to hold the door open for exiting lawyers from the last case. With a polite nod and his customary I-know-something-you-don't-know smile at the room in general, he seated himself behind Rep and Melissa.

The clerk called *United States versus Clevenger.* Finnegan, six feet tall, trim and wiry with short black hair, strode briskly to the appellant's table. Two lawyers Rep didn't recognize took seats on the other side. The professionally courteous smile Finnegan flashed at them scarcely softened a mocking glint in his lively blue eyes. Kuchinski kept his seat in the front row of the gallery.

"May it please the Court," Finnegan said a nanosecond after the presiding judge nodded at him. "The only issue—"

"Counsel, what is this case doing in federal court?"

This question, from a dour jurist at the presiding judge's left, clearly came as no surprise to Finnegan. He slipped seamlessly from his prepared argument to a crisp exposition of the crime-on-the-high-seas theory.

"I'm not asking why you *could* bring it, but why you *did*. Why stretch so outlandishly for federal jurisdiction over a garden-variety state law offense?"

Finnegan had barely started on the strong federal interest in the country's navigable waters when the third judge interrupted him.

"Counsel, do you feel that erroneous exercise of prosecutorial discretion, if indeed it was erroneous, is jurisdictional?" She pretended that this was a question to Finnegan, but every lawyer in the room recognized it as a barbed comment aimed at her dour colleague.

"I do not. The ground for dismissal here was lack of subject matter jurisdiction, and with the court's permission I will turn to that issue now."

Finnegan segued back into his prepared argument. Over the next fourteen minutes he got exactly one more question—"Where is that in the record, counsel?" After he reserved the rest of his time for rebuttal and sat down, the older and heavier of Clevenger's lawyers went to the podium.

"Whatever Jimmy Clevenger may be, he isn't a pirate. If every word in the indictment is true, he would at most be arguably guilty of a crime under Wisconsin law, implicating no substantial federal interest. There is simply no excuse for literally making a federal case out of this. That is—"

"What if he had actually raped the victim?" the third judge asked. "Would that be chargeable under the piracy statute?"

"No. Rape is a state law crime."

"So is armed robbery. But armed robbery on the high seas is piracy, and the same guys who wrote the Constitution didn't think twice about hanging people for it under federal law."

"Robbery is 'depredation,' which is the term the piracy statute uses."

"And rape isn't?"

"It is not," the lawyer said amidst indignant gasps from the activists. "'Depredation' involves pillaging, which requires the forcible taking of goods."

"So if the defendant had used the threat of force to swipe a beer from a cooler on deck the government could legitimately have charged him with piracy, but threatening the victim with forcible rape doesn't meet the statutory standard—is that your argument, counsel?"

"I didn't write the statute, your honor. The men who did knew how to say 'assault and battery' or 'sexual assault' when that was what they meant, and they chose not to include those offenses in this law."

"So what you're saying," the presiding judge interjected, his eyes twinkling as if this were cocktail party repartee, "is that there must be a threat to property, not person?"

"Not just a threat, your Honor. An actual deprivation by force."

"Or by the threat of force?"

"Well, yes, the threat of force can be enough."

Rep straightened in alert attention, the way he did when a pitcher with a three-run lead went two-oh on the leadoff hitter in the eighth. Melissa noticed, and saw Valerie Clevenger doing the same thing. She wondered why. For his part, Rep wondered whether Clevenger's lawyer had heard the air whistling past his ears as he dropped through the trap door.

"Doesn't the indictment allege that here?" the presiding judge asked.

"It does not. It alleges overreaction to jocular banter during a run-of-the-mill sexual proposition."

"'Jocular banter?'" the third judge demanded. "'Sex or swim?' On Lake Michigan, near midnight, almost half-a-mile from shore?"

"Even interpreted in the worst possible light, that comment threatened the victim's honor—not her property. She was not deprived of any *property*."

For the briefest of moments the presiding judge allowed himself what, if he had been anything but a judge, would have been a smile. Leaning forward with his left hand cupped around his chin he asked innocently:

"What about the boat, counsel?"

"Excuse me, your Honor?"

"The sailboat, the ship, the watercraft. According to the indictment, when the victim dove overboard the defendant was left in possession and control of the ship."

"The ship was back in the victim's possession within two hours."

"So what? Isn't the victim's use of her own ship for two hours a valuable property right?"

The lawyer knew he had no good answer. 'No' would be silly, and 'yes' would start him down a slippery slope, with no place to stop before the bottom.

"Not in the context of the facts alleged here," he finally said. "A clear and present threat of death or serious physical injury is one thing, and a clumsy, frat-boy come-on is something else."

He paused, visibly bracing himself for a blistering challenge from the third judge. The next question, however, came from the dour judge, the one who had started out on Clevenger's side.

"Counsel, isn't that a jury question?"

There wasn't much after that, and what there was struck Rep as anticlimactic. After a limp finish by Clevenger's lawyer and a brisk rebuttal from Finnegan, the presiding judge said the court would take the case under advisement. A general exodus began. Rep tracked Kuchinski down and dusted off a couple of the encouraging bromides lawyers resort to after getting smoked by an appellate panel.

"Aggressive questioning by the court is often a positive sign."

"Yeah, right. We're lucky they didn't reverse from the bench. I wonder how those California boys will like Milwaukee in February, because we could be right back in front of a jury in two months. I've gotta go listen to the dream-teamers spin me about taking this to the Supreme Court."

Rep turned to Melissa but found that Clevenger had intercepted her.

"Professor Pennyworth, could I have a word with you?"

"Certainly."

The two women moved toward the long, frosted glass and maple wall fronting the clerk's domain. (Calling the sumptuous quarters of the Clerk of the United States Court of Appeals for the Seventh Circuit an "office" would be like calling San Simeon "a house.") Melissa spotted Hoeckstra cruising down the hallway with damn-the-torpedoes body language. Mignon trailed her, making determined but unsuccessful efforts to catch her attention. Clevenger waited until Hoeckstra was well past before she spoke.

"Were you and your husband planning on going back to Milwaukee this afternoon?"

"No, we're going to spend the weekend in Chicago. Professor Angstrom is at a symposium at Notre Dame on the Pius controversy, trying to stir up interest. I may run over to South Bend tomorrow to see how he's doing."

"Then I wonder if I could ask you a great favor. It looks like we're going to lose this appeal and have to try Jimmy's case again.

I need to talk with you about something. Can I buy you a drink around two o'clock this afternoon?"

"Sure. We're at the Hilton. Shall we meet in the bar there?"

"I'd prefer a place called Spirits of Chicago about two blocks away. For reasons I'll explain, I want to avoid the Hilton until we've had our talk."

"Spirits of Chicago. Got it. I'll see you at two."

"Thank you. I can't tell you how much I appreciate this."

Clevenger scurried off. Melissa found her way back to Rep and told him about her request.

"I didn't see how I could decently refuse," she said apologetically.

"You couldn't. If I'd spent half-a-million dollars on lawyers who were about to get me right back where I started, I'd probably want to talk to someone who didn't have a law degree myself."

"Take me to lunch and you can do exactly that."

Chapter Seventeen

"Nothing quite like a crisp sauterne in the afternoon, is there?" Clevenger asked at eight minutes after two.

"I'm a sauterne virgin, but it's quite good," Melissa said.

"Down to business. I'm meeting with Professor Angstrom this evening."

"I thought he'd be in South Bend all weekend."

"He's driving over to Chicago just for the meeting. He has implied that he has information that could be extremely helpful to Jimmy. I need to know how reliable he is."

Melissa took a deliberate sip before responding. *Too bad Mignon isn't here. He'd answer that question without mincing words.*

"For me to give you an answer that will be of any use to you," she said after this pause, "what I say would have to be completely confidential."

"Understood. I won't even tell Jimmy's lawyers that you're the source."

"Very well, then. Let me put it this way. I don't think Angstrom will tell you an out-and-out lie. But I wouldn't rely on anything he said unless you can verify it independently. If you parse his statements they tend to be literally true. But they often create a false impression—especially if he has a personal interest in creating that impression."

"Like money, for example."

"Or professional score-settling or status. But mostly money, yes."

Melissa then gave Clevenger an academic insider's account of Angstrom's Villa Terrace performance. She described the viciousness of the trap he'd laid for Mignon, and the unlovely combination of glee and gratuitous cruelty with which he'd sprung it. Imagining how she'd feel if her son were facing prison, Melissa couldn't help being impressed by Clevenger's focus and professional detachment as she scribbled notes and asked precise questions.

"Would you excuse me for a few minutes?" she asked then. "I need to discuss something with Jimmy's lawyers before I take the next step."

"Sure," Melissa said.

Clevenger got up and walked, coatless, out onto the restaurant's smoking plaza, overlooking the Chicago River. She paced back and forth before the window, smoking in a desultory way and chatting on a cell-phone. After four minutes she put out her cigarette and headed back inside.

"You've been very kind," she said as she sat back down. "I hate to impose further, but I wonder if I might give you a little detailed background about my son. Knowing the whole story might make it easier for you to remember something about Angstrom that could prove critical."

"Of course," Melissa said. "The only other thing I'd be doing is grading papers in a hotel room while my husband returns phone calls and marks up a trademark license agreement."

Over the next forty-five minutes they finished their wine, had another glass, and switched to tea. Clevenger was setting down a porcelain cup when for the first time she seemed close to losing the tight grip on her emotions.

"I understand how you could take 'sex or swim' two ways. But you've seen Jimmy. He can't do hard-as-nails. He's the kind of kid who gets drinks dumped in his lap on Brady Street if he comes on too strong."

"But Hoeckstra didn't slap his face. She jumped and swam for it."

"That's what I can't figure out. Would you mind stopping up in my room back at the Hilton for a couple of minutes so I can show you something? That's what I wanted to clear with Jimmy's lawyers when I stepped outside."

Melissa stifled a groan and mentally rebuked herself for her impatience. She hadn't bargained for two hours of chick-chat, but she was talking to a woman who had nothing in her life but a demanding job and her only child. As serious as the sex-or-swim case was for Jimmy Clevenger, Melissa thought, it was a life-and-death matter for his mother. Bill paid and tip left, they bundled themselves against the cold and bustled out into the twilit chill, like knights leading a sortie from a besieged castle. The morning's brave sun was now a distant memory as the gloaming enveloped them. The winter solstice approached. It would be pitch black by four-fifteen.

"What I want to show you is something Angstrom sent me."

"A tease?"

"He called it 'a sampler.' I deliberately left it in my room this morning because I didn't want a federal marshal to stumble over it while he was going through my briefcase at the security checkpoint."

"I'll be happy to come up."

Clevenger's room looked exactly like Rep and Melissa's, except for the sturdy glass ashtrays on the desk and the bedside table. In less than three minutes, Melissa found herself seated in the room's wing chair with a glass of ice and a bottle of Aqua Fina on the window sill beside her and a photocopy of a single page in her hands. It was on the letterhead of the United States Department of Justice, addressed to someone identified as the general counsel for Goettinger Corporation. It said that the United States had completed its inquiries into the matter in question and was closing its file without contemplation of further proceedings. Dated September 12, 2003, it was signed by Terence Finnegan.

"Do you know whether this is genuine?"

"Yes. I've seen the original. I billed Goettinger Corporation over sixty-thousand dollars to get that letter written."

"So Angstrom is implying that he knows something else—something a bit more sinister."

"That's my read," Clevenger said. "What I have to decide is whether I can trust him."

"Well, as the Irish say, 'God is good, but don't dance in a small boat.'"

An authoritative rap sounded at the door. Melissa automatically glanced at her watch. Ten after four. Clevenger opened the door to two men in suits and one in a blazer.

"Charlie Simmons, Hilton security," the blazer said. "These two gentlemen are Chicago police detectives. They'd like to speak with you."

"About what?"

"Harald Angstrom," the taller of the two suits said. "He's dead."

"What? Dead? Forgive me, but that's quite a shock. I was expecting to meet him later this evening."

"We know."

"I guess you'd better come in."

They did. Melissa stayed where she was. She expected to be told to leave very soon, and under the circumstances she thought it prudent to wait for that instruction.

"How did he die?" Clevenger asked.

"Poison. Curare sprayed in his mouth."

"Suicide?"

"Set up to look that way, but we don't think so."

"When did this happen?"

"Well," the shorter suit said, "a little over three hours ago he was in South Bend, Indiana, which is at least seventy-five minutes from Chicago on a good day, not counting toll booths. That means he could have gotten here by two-thirty or so—say two-twenty if he really hustled and caught every light once he left the freeway. An anonymous citizen phoned in a tip about an hour ago about a body in a Prius, and the body turned out to be Angstrom. So we figure it happened between two-twenty and three-fifteen."

"How can you pin-point the time he was in South Bend so precisely?" Clevenger asked. "I'm sorry, you're here to ask me questions, not the other way around."

"That question we don't mind answering," the taller suit said. "This is how we know. We found it on the front seat of the car, beside the body."

Clevenger gingerly took a page in a glassine paper-protector. Melissa stepped forward to examine it discreetly over her shoulder. It was a print-out of an email:

CLEVENGER, VALERIE

FROM: Valerie Clevenger [vclevenger@wi.rr.com]
SENT: Friday, December 14, 2007, 1:10 p.m.
TO: Angstrom, Harald S. [hsa@uwm.edu]
SUBJECT: Meeting

Professor Angstrom,

Responding to your message, I will be happy to meet with you in Chicago at the time you suggested. I'm staying at the Hilton on Wacker. Show this message to the concierge and have me paged if you can't reach me on the house phone.

Valerie Clevenger

"One-ten in Chicago would be two-ten in South Bend," the taller suit said, "but he'd pick up the hour difference traveling west. It's after four here now, so that's where the three hours comes from."

"Got it," Clevenger said.

The shorter suit glanced up at Melissa.

"And who might you be, ma'am?" he asked.

"I'm Melissa Seton Pennyworth," she said. "And I might be a witness."

◇◇◇

Just about two hours later Melissa lay, fully clothed, over the covers on the bed in the hotel room she shared with Rep. He was no longer returning phone calls or marking up a trademark license agreement. He was looking thoughtfully toward the blank screen of a television.

"This does make the cheese more binding, doesn't it?" he said.

"I screwed up," Melissa said woodenly. "It wasn't just academic shenanigans. My premise was wrong."

"My premise, actually. If we're going to berate ourselves all night, I want my share of credit for the screw-up."

"Our premise. The point is that Angstrom wasn't just pulling some *Mean Girls*-stunt on Mignon. He was doing something that led to murder."

"That doesn't mean anything would be different if you'd dropped a dime on Tereska Bleifert."

"Maybe not. But now it's clear she knows something important that she hasn't told anybody so far. Whoever murdered Angstrom might have other targets in mind, and Bleifert's information may help protect them."

"So did you give her name to the police when they questioned you in Clevenger's room?" Rep asked.

"No. Might as well give a rosary to an atheist. You should have seen Bleifert when Hoeckstra confronted her. If a couple of cops try a Mutt-and-Jeff routine on her all they're going to get is a face-full of Polish attitude."

"What are you going to do, then?"

"Talk to her myself."

"Just because you can wrap me around your little finger doesn't mean you're magic," Rep said. "Do you really think you can get her to tell you things she won't tell the cops?"

"Yep."

"How?"

"Gray lies."

"Meaning what?"

Melissa told him what she had in mind.

"Ouch," he said.

"Yep."

Chapter Eighteen

"Hi, Stan, this is Rep Pennyworth, " Rep was saying ten minutes later to the voice-mail of Stanley Watkins, assistant general counsel of Medea Press. "This is a little off the wall, but it could be important. If Medea has gotten a pitch over the transom in the last three months or so for an action/adventure novel featuring an intrepid academic with a religious-historical document as the McGuffin, I'd appreciate it if you'd give me a call."

A knock sounded at the door while he was signing off.

"That'll be Walt," Melissa said as she went to answer it. Kuchinski had made it into the room and accepted a Miller Genuine Draft from the room bar by the time Rep finished leaving the same message on the voice-mail of another New York publishing contact—his fourth so far.

"That's a little compulsive, isn't it, boy? Still cranking out billable work after seven o'clock on Friday night?"

"If I find a way to bill this I'll officially become the leading rainmaker in the American Bar Association. I'm just looking for food to feed the beast."

"Boone Fletcher," Melissa said in response to Kuchinski's quizzical look.

"I heard about that. You can finally call yourself a real lawyer now. You've been threatened by a reporter."

"I'm not sure I'd call it a threat," Rep said. "More of an insinuation."

"It was a threat," Melissa said. "'Play ball with me or see your name in boldface type under ugly headlines.'"

"I take it that wouldn't go over particularly well with your partners back in Indianapolis."

"It would not. The firm's policy is that a partner's name should only appear in the business section or before the words 'declined to comment.'"

"So you're thinking you might buy a little favor with Boone if you can show that Angstrom and Gates were incipient competitors?"

"It's a fresh angle with a local twist. Besides, I haven't come up with anything else yet. No cop would believe Gates killed a wannabe just to reduce the competition, but a reporter might."

"I 'spose. Most reporters I know will believe anything but the truth."

Rep and Melissa pulled on their coats and the three of them began their four-block trek to the Wabash Steak House.

"Threat, insinuation, or something else, it's not a bad idea to accommodate the Boone-ster," Kuchinski said. "It'd be nice to find out what that boy knows before he puts it in the paper if we're going to try the sex-or-swim case again. And he won't show us his unless we show him ours."

"Wouldn't it be pushing the outside of the envelope for him to give information to one side in a case he's covering for his paper?" Melissa asked.

"If Boone Fletcher smells a Pulitzer Prize it won't be question of pushing the outside of the envelope," Kuchinski said. "He won't even stay in the mailbox. What's a McGuffin, by the way?"

"It's something arbitrarily valuable that triggers the action in a story because people want to get their hands on it," Melissa said.

"Like the letters of transit in *Casablanca*," Rep added.

"Or this supposed papal order in Taylor Gates' next story," Kuchinski said. "Got it."

"You know something?" Rep said. "I'm having trouble buying that. A buddy at Saint Philomena Press told me he turned down a mystery where the murder revolved around competition between

two college football coaches to recruit a star defensive end. He
said, 'You don't kill someone over a defensive end. A quarterback
who can throw a tight spiral eighty yards against the wind and
split the wide-out's hands with it—maybe. But not a defensive
end.' That papal order strikes me as falling in the defensive end
category of McGuffins."

"I'm not so sure," Kuchinski said. "You're the pop-culture
maven, professor. What do you think? If Gates could start a
rumor that his next masterpiece is based on a genuine historic
document that just came to light and has the History Channel
all excited, would that jump-start sales?"

"It might. Say you were writing a mystery based on the O. J.
Simpson murder case. You could make up an affidavit by some
hit-man, written just before he dies, saying that he killed the
two victims and framed Simpson because Simpson had backed
out of a deal or something."

"Sounds dime-a-dozen so far," Rep said.

"Maybe. But say that when the book is about to come out
the tabloids start running stories saying it's based on fact. Say
those stories talk about bomb threats to the publisher, suppressed
FBI reports, and that type of thing."

"Like the gas attack at Villa Terrace," Rep said.

"Except not as lame."

"I think the real-world tie-in makes all the difference,"
Kuchinski said. "With a hook like that, something like the
Simpson story would have a shot. Without it, that thing would
bounce back faster than the trial court's dismissal of the indictment in this case is going to."

"The post-argument de-briefing didn't change your mind?"
Rep asked.

"The left-coasters decided it was fifty-fifty. Those are the
same geniuses who picked the jury consultant, so I'll stick with
my prediction this morning."

"Speaking of that high-priced jury consulting firm," **Rep**
said, "did it ever come up with any explanation for going so far
off the rails?"

"Yeah: It was all the lawyers' fault."

"Isn't it always?"

"They talked after the trial to every juror they could. And they interviewed three let's-pretend jurors they'd hired to shadow the trial while it was going on. Their official conclusion was that our jury went into deliberations with at least three strong partisans for our side, but they got frustrated because they didn't feel we'd given them enough ammunition to counter the arguments of the jurors who favored conviction."

"That seems a little…generic," Rep said.

"Well, if I'd just been paid humpty-thousand dollars for a wrong answer I'd tend to get a mite generic myself."

They stepped into the Wabash Steak House and gratefully left the biting wind behind them. They discovered that the restaurant had not only remembered their reservations but could actually honor them and provide a table immediately. They were passing around dinner rolls and menus when Melissa brought the jury consultant up again.

"Your comment about shadow jurors intrigued me," she said. "I assumed the main thing a jury consulting firm did was tell you what kind of jurors you want for your case. And that always puzzled me, because you shouldn't have to pay someone to tell you that you wanted twelve libidinous frat boys in something like the sex-or-swim case."

"It involves more big words than that," Rep said.

"Jury consultants actually do three main things," Kuchinski said. "First, they show a heavily condensed summary of the evidence to a cross-section of the community that matches the jury you're likely to get, so you can see how that mock-jury reacts. Second, they put shadow jurors in the courtroom and tell you day by day how those people are reacting to what they've heard. And third, they dress it all up with jargon like 'passive/alienated' and 'aggressive/reactive' and chart data points on quadrants in a graph so that it looks scientific enough to justify a gigantic price-tag. That's what Rep meant by more big words."

"But why do smart people pay high prices for flimflam-mery?"

"Because the jury consultants are usually right," Rep said.

"Hmm," Melissa said.

"Try the bone-in ribeye," Kuchinski said. "It's delicious."

Chapter Nineteen

"I don't consider this smoking," Melissa heard Bleifert say to a twenty-something male sharing a table with her at the Cairo Café, just off Downer Avenue. Melissa guessed, correctly, that the male was Grady Schoenfeld.

Bleifert put a hookah's plastic tube between her lips, drew dreamily on it, then blew a lazy stream of white smoke toward the ceiling.

"Right. I don't know why anyone would call that smoking."

"Try it."

Taking the tube from her with a good-sport shrug, he took a puff.

"It's milder and cooler," he said. "But it's still tobacco smoke, even if it's peach flavored."

Melissa walked over to them. A week had gone by since Angstrom's murder. She had wanted to let a decent interval pass after Angstrom's memorial service at UWM on Tuesday before approaching Bleifert. She shook her head now, stunned by the resilience of youth. Bleifert had sobbed at the memorial service and hadn't shown up for class or work on Wednesday. Two days later she still wasn't exactly lighthearted, but she was teasing and flirting and cultivating bad habits—like a normal nineteen-year old.

"Oh, hi, professor," Bleifert said, glancing up at Melissa and then nodding toward the hookah. "Have you ever tried this?"

"Yes, except not with tobacco."

"Pot?" Schoenfeld asked in an astonished voice.

"Yes. College students sometimes smoked marijuana, even in the olden days."

"I didn't mean it like that."

"Yeah, he did, actually," Bleifert said, giving Schoenfeld a joshing little nudge. "Would you like to, you know, sit down or something?"

"If you don't mind," Melissa said, ignoring Schoenfeld' imperfectly suppressed sigh. "I ordered some tea at the counter and I was hoping to chat while I drank it."

"Do you want to try a hit?" Bleifert asked, proffering the tube.

Melissa considered playing along just to seem companionable but decided against it. She figured she'd look like a phony, and she was afraid she'd cough like an eighth-grader trying her first Camel Light.

"No, thanks."

Bad move. Bleifert's mood swung like politician's after a surprising poll.

"So this isn't a social encounter, huh?"

"I'm not sure what you mean."

"Look, I'll save you some time, okay? I got to Professor Angstrom's office within half-an-hour after the Villa Terrace panel ended. I used a key he'd given me to go in and return the Power Point stuff. I only turned on one light, but it was enough to see the mess. I tried to call him, then ended up running all over the building looking for a guard so that I could report the break-in. I should have just gone straight to the security desk, but I thought I could find a guard making his rounds. By the time I finally gave up and did go to the desk, there was no guard there—apparently because he'd gone off with you. So I left my name and number at the desk and I took off, because I wanted to hook up with McHunk here. And yes, I was at Notre

Dame for the same symposium Professor Angstrom attended, and no, I didn't hide in his car and kill him after he'd driven to Chicago."

"My mother warned me that I looked severe in hunter green," Melissa said, "but I didn't expect you to take me for Torquemada."

"Grand inquisitor," Bleifert said to Schoenfeld.

"I *know* who Torquemada was," Schoenfeld said, with a trace of affectionate exasperation.

Schoenfeld struck Melissa as a little bland, maybe a bit too anxious to please. His hair was cut like a novice Rotarian's, and his pale blue eyes behind wire-rims were half-hidden by heavy lids, as if he couldn't be bothered to open them all the way. Not a bad looking kid, but no one's idea of McHunk—unless you were gazing at him through infatuated eyes. Was he the first guy who'd ever been nice to Bleifert? The first one not scared off by her brains and her sharp tongue?

Bleifert's gaze snapped back to Melissa.

"Don't try to game me, okay? The whole point of the Cairo Café is hookahs, and you don't smoke but you're here at the same time I am. Don't tell me it's coincidence."

"Hardly. I checked with four or five people, made a list of half-a-dozen places near campus where I'd have a good shot of running into you, and Cairo Café was at the top."

"And you did that because Li asked you to have a discreet little chat with me to help him decide whether one of his coeds is a murderer so he can get to work on damage control, right?"

A waitress in a modified chador set a steaming cup of green tea in front of Melissa, who took a tentative sip. Bleifert had a point about the hookahs. Melissa couldn't imagine anyone coming to the Cairo Café for its tea.

"I have an ulterior motive, but interrogation isn't it. Being lured into a stairwell and trapped there like an airhead in a romance novel wasn't exactly a highlight of the semester for me, but I'm not conducting my own private investigation into the incident."

Melissa choked down another throatful of tea while pink crept up the backs of Bleifert's ears.

"Then why did you go to so much trouble to track me down?"

"For starters, I wanted to return something to you." Fishing the holy card from her purse, Melissa tendered it to Bleifert.

"Two!" Schoenfeld said, making a referee's count-it signal with his right hand as Bleifert accepted the card.

"Yep," Bleifert said gamely. "Burned my ass for sure."

"You dropped it at Villa Terrace. I thought you'd want it back."

"I do. Thanks. Sorry for the bitch act just now. Since Professor Angstrom's murder I've been acting like Paris Hilton during a Midol shortage."

"Actually, I'm the one who should be thanking you."

"Why is that?

"Seeing my name on that card reminded me of one of the only times I've cried since I grew up."

"Whoa," Bleifert said.

"I was home from college during spring break, and my mother asked me to go over to Saint Peters Church, near where we lived in Kansas City, to pick up my grandmother who was there for Lenten devotions. I walked in about three minutes after the service was over. And in the front pew I saw about twelve girls in parochial school uniforms praying in unison. All at once I realized that they were praying for me."

"Huh?" Schoenfeld demanded.

Bleifert gave Schoenfeld a brisk rundown about Lenten prayers for lapsed Catholics.

"Right," Melissa confirmed. "These girls had never heard of me but they were giving up an hour on a Friday afternoon to pray for me and try to save my soul. Suddenly, before I realized what was happening, tears were streaming down my cheeks."

"And Terry's card reminded you of that," Schoenfeld said, nodding his head in contented understanding. "Cool."

"Not only your card but a couple of things you said when we talked about my agnosticism. I fell away from the Church in my teens—fell a long, *long* way from it. But the more I thought about what you'd said, the more I wondered if I hadn't given the Church enough of a chance."

No actress alive could have faked the transformation that swept over Bleifert. Every ounce of chip-on-her-shoulder attitude evaporated from her features. Her eyes widened and lit up. Her lips split in a delighted smile. Her face seemed to glow as she eagerly leaned forward.

'*Gray lie' hell*, Melissa thought. *I am scum under a rock.*

"That's wonderful," Bleifert said.

"I'm not really sure where to take it from here. I was wondering if you know a priest at the Newman Center on campus who might be a good one for me to talk to about—I don't know, about exploring my feelings further."

"That might be risky until you have tenure," Bleifert said. "A lot of your colleagues would think you'd gone over to the dark side if they spotted you traipsing into the Newman Center."

"I hope you're wrong about that," Melissa said.

"The priest I know best is a Franciscan at Saint Josephats, the basilica on the south side. If you like, I'd be happy to call him and try to get you in touch with him."

"That would be very thoughtful. I'd appreciate it."

"I could also get you some books. Oh, God, I'm coming off like a Jehovah's Witness, aren't I?"

"Why don't we start with one book?" Melissa suggested, smiling. "I wouldn't want to over-commit on required reading."

"You'll have it Monday morning."

"Thanks. I'll leave you two to enjoy the rest of your evening together."

As Melissa was leaving, she heard Bleifert and Schoenfeld fall effortlessly into carefree banter.

"Okay, explain *that one*, McSkeptic."

"I'm happy that you're happy, my Polish princess, but one grace-filled moment doesn't erase all the horrible things that have been done in the name of religion over the centuries."

"Hitler, Stalin, Mao."

"Come again?"

"Two atheists and a pagan," Bleifert said with a fierce and triumphant intensity. "And among them they managed in about forty years to kill more people by several orders of magnitude than all the Crusades and all the jihads and all the pograms and all the inquisitions and all the witch-hunts in history, even if you take it back to the annihilation of the Midianites by the Israelites in Numbers."

A pause of three or four seconds ensued, as if Schoenfeld were catching his breath after this verbal assault.

"Well, yeah," he conceded then. "But they had better *technology*."

PART THREE

Scribbling On the Tabula Rasa

"Behavioral researchers have attempted to understand what kinds of jurors reach what types of decisions and how attitudes affect the way in which jurors must be informed and persuaded toward a particular view in a trial. Jurors do not come into the courtroom with a blank slate or tabula rasa. They bring with them a large number of attitudes which are firmly entrenched in their minds."

—Donald Vinson, *Jury Trials: The Psychology of Winning Strategy*

Chapter Twenty

The third Saturday in December, 2007

"You owe me big time, Mr. Pennyworth."

That's what I get for turning my cell-phone on before eight o'clock in the morning on a weekend.

"Owe you for what, Frank?" Rep asked, reluctantly laying his *Milwaukee Journal Sentinel* next to a bowl of corn flakes now doomed to soggy limpness well before he could taste them.

"For going well above and beyond the call of duty."

"For an editor at a New York publishing house to be at his desk before nine a.m. on a weekday would qualify as heroic," Rep said, adding an hour for eastern time. "On a weekend it's transcendent. This is about my query a while back?"

"Yes. And coming into my office isn't the heroic part. I'm calling you from my squalid, thirty-two-hundred square foot garret in Tribeca."

"By all means get to the heroism. Did a pitch or a story like the one I described come in over the transom?"

"No. I checked the junior readers and came up empty. But I didn't stop there. I showed some initiative. I put the word out because the professor-in-Milwaukee part rang a very faint bell. It turns out we did get a 'script from a tweedy-type in Milwaukee named Harald Angstrom. But it didn't come in over any transom."

"You mean he had an agent?"

"Not just *an* agent, buddy. Amy Lee. It hit the desk of a senior editor maybe four months ago, and it hit with a very loud thud. The buzz isn't supposed to start for another six months, but it's a go."

"Even though Angstrom has passed away? "

"You kidding? That's hype-fodder, not a buzz-killer—a fantastic hook. Getting murdered may be this egghead's greatest career move."

"My word," Rep said. "Religious/mystical thriller with an intrepid and omni-competent academic as the hero?"

"Not even close. Courtroom drama revolving around complex machinations in jury selection. Don't ask for more because I had to take a colleague to lunch at *Nouvelle Justine* just to get that much—and that place creeps me out."

"You're right. I owe you."

"You bet you do. When the next John Grisham stumbles into your office wondering whether he needs permission to equip his query letter with a computer chip that will play the *Perry Mason Theme* when it's opened, I want to hear about it first."

"You shall. "

Rep scribbled *Frank Thompkins/Artemis Books* in white space at the top of the *Journal Sentinel's* front page. By happenstance, he wrote the words immediately above the headline announcing:

'SEX OR SWIM' DISMISSAL REVERSED
CASE SENT BACK FOR RETRIAL

◇◇◇

"Thank you for calling back," Melissa said less than forty minutes later as, baffled, she watched Rep bustling around the bedroom. "Could you hold on for just a minute?" Then, to Rep, "You're not going into the office are you?"

"Yep."

"A little after eight-thirty on a Saturday?"

"I'd be there already except that Walt won't be in until nine."

"*Walt* is coming in on a Saturday?"

"Has to. Q Kasmaryck seems to have gotten into a scrape of some kind early this morning."

Melissa put the phone back to her ear.

"I'm sorry, Father Huebner. My husband was turning into a blur and I thought I'd better find out what was happening. It's very thoughtful of you to call on a Saturday with Christmas only a week away."

"We're as busy as H and R Block would be in April if it filled out tax forms for free," her caller's reedy, tenor voice said. "But this is important. If you can possibly get out to Mount Mary College about three o'clock this afternoon, I should have an hour between two commitments out there."

"I'll be there. How will I know you?"

"I'll be the one in the papal tiara."

"Um, *okay.* "

"No, seriously," Father Gregory Huebner, O.F.M. said. "Papal tiara."

"I'll tell you one thing, if she was gonna throw an all-night party on a yacht during the Fourth of July fireworks, she should have made damn good and sure she knew everyone she let on that boat. That was just asking for it."

"We're not supposed to consider that, though."

"I know, I'm just saying."

Rep had to work hard to keep his attention focused on the grainy figures, videotaped through one-way mirrors, who populated his computer screen. The first speaker looked like he was in his mid-sixties, with scattered white hair and liver-spotted hands. The second, a woman, had silver-streaked black hair pulled back and tied in what Rep guessed was supposed to be a pony tail. They were two of the seventeen people that Jurimetrics, Inc. had gathered last summer to help the Clevenger defense team figure out what would happen when they tried the sex-or-swim case.

It looked like Jurimetrics had come pretty close to the cross-section the exercise required. Several retirees, a postal worker, someone described generically as a "civil servant," a couple of homemakers, an office manager—that was the woman with the attempted pony tail—two pink-collar types, a bespectacled, poker-faced guy in his late twenties who said he was self-employed, three students with purple and green streaks in their hair, a machinist, a construction worker, two public school teachers—and Harald Angstrom. You didn't get investment bankers or doctors to give up a Saturday for the stipend Jurimetrics paid, of course, but they weren't too likely to show up on juries, either. Three African-Americans, two Hispanics, the rest white. Ten women and seven men.

A hand-printed white label on the plastic DVD case next to Rep's computer read: CLEVENGER JURY ANALYSIS STIMULUS I THROUGH V. Rep had watched Stimulus I and Stimulus II, each a fifteen minute speech by a lawyer summarizing and arguing the evidence, one from the prosecution perspective and one from the defense side. Now he was watching the seventeen mock-jurors discuss the case under the impact of these two "stimuli." He found the discussion bracing, as would anyone who imagined that his fate might one day lie in the hands of a jury:

"What did she invite him onto the yacht for? Parcheesi?

"She didn't invite him on to rape her."

"But he didn't rape her."

"He tried to."

"No he didn't either. He didn't even *touch* her."

"I thought he did. I thought that one lawyer said—"

"No. He said there was 'no physical mistreatment.' I wrote that down."

"That's not the point, though. The point is, did he threaten her?"

"Yeah, 'cause I think if all it was was a threat, he'd just get a small fine or maybe thirty days or something."

"'Sex or swim' isn't a threat. It's just something you say."

"Why would she jump in the drink if she wasn't threatened?"

"Maybe she was high."

"Yeah, these rich kids today, they do blow like we did beer."

"How do you know that? About her, I mean."

"Maybe she overreacted."

"Maybe she's just a crazy chick. You know, guilting herself over sex or something, so the guy says some dumb thing and she freaks."

"No, you know what, I can't see that." This from the office manager. "The woman jumped into *Lake Michigan* and swam *half-a-mile.* How can you say she didn't feel threatened?"

"Maybe she *felt* threatened, but that doesn't mean she *was* threatened. I mean, what says the guy meant it that way?"

"I wish we had more information."

"Well, the cops thought he meant it. FBI or whoever."

"But we're not supposed to consider that."

"I know, I'm just saying. Those guys are professionals. They know what they're doing. My nephew is a criminology major, and he says the stuff they can do in those labs is amazing."

"That's right. Like, this one time on *C.S.I.*—"

"No lab can tell you what was in this kid's head."

"Which kid?"

"Either of them."

"What's 'threat' supposed to mean, anyway? Does anyone have a dictionary?"

And so on for almost forty-five minutes. Relevant and insightful comments interspersed with stuff so off-the-wall it made your gut churn. They finally took a vote. Twelve for conviction, five for acquittal.

Hmm. At this stage, Rep knew, Jurimetrics wasn't shooting for a definitive prediction. It was trying to find out which themes worked with which types of jurors. Kuchinski hadn't given Rep the written analysis for this first round, but Rep could guess what it said: Clevenger would have initial partisans on the jury, but they'd probably be weaker personalities, easily led. They'd need something solid to grab onto if they were going to hold out against the hard-liners more viscerally sympathetic to the prosecution theory.

Sighing, Rep watched Stimulus III and Stimulus IV. A not-that-young woman with a heavy Boston accent was pretending to be Carolyn Hoeckstra going through direct and cross-examinations. The direct was straightforward, although the lawyer doing it wasn't anything like as good as Finnegan. The cross started out making obvious points, playing to defense themes that had worked well in Stimulus I:

He didn't have a weapon of any kind?

No.

He didn't force his way onto the boat?

No.

He didn't hit you?

No.

Didn't grab your breasts?

No.

In fact he didn't touch your breasts, did he?

No.

Or your buttocks?

No.

Didn't try to kiss you?

Not really.

Then came a couple of zingers:

You aren't married, are you?

Not any more. Not for over a year.

But you're on a prescription medication called Enovid?

Yes.

Which is a birth control pill?

Yes.

How long have you been using birth control on a regular basis?

Since I was fifteen.

Rep gaped. No way they could have dreamed of getting that stuff into evidence. But if you know what works, sometimes you can suggest it and sneak into a juror's head without actually presenting it as evidence. And sometimes one juror is all it takes.

Did you ever hear of a contest called BAD?

Yes.

What did BAD stand for?

"Best Ass at Downer."

That would be Downer High School on the East Side of Milwaukee?

Yes.

That was a contest where a number of students at Downer High had their naked buttocks shown on a computer site, and other students...voted which one was best?

Yes.

This was voluntary?

Yes.

Did you take part?

I finished third.

That rang a bell. They'd somehow gotten part of that in. They'd had to work hard to do it, and now Rep understood why they'd made the effort.

He clicked to the discussion following these additions to the mock jury's information. It was much shorter. The BAD stuff made the office manager furious at the defense, but the students giggled. The vote this time was ten to seven—still for conviction.

Stimulus V. The screen this time showed a woman with a big JURIMETRICS tag on her chest, to make it clear that she wasn't one of the lawyers and she wasn't playing a role; she was a neutral. She stood at the podium holding a single piece of paper.

"Would it have any impact on your deliberations if you were told that, before this case was brought to trial in federal court, Carolyn Hoeckstra's complaint to the Milwaukee Police Department the date of the incident was reviewed by a special prosecutor appointed by the Attorney General of the State of Wisconsin, and that prosecutor decided not to proceed with a criminal complaint against Mr. Clevenger?"

That was the whole stimulus. Rep clicked impatiently to the discussion. He couldn't believe that this had flipped the mock jurors, but it must have. The discussion quickly ran out of steam. Another vote: Nine-eight for conviction.

Huh? Jury consulting firms sometimes make wrong calls. But a wrong call is one thing, and mistaking a toss-up for a slam dunk is something else. Jurimetrics couldn't possibly have looked at these discussions and these votes and told Clevenger's lawyers they were sure to win.

Rep had to kill half-an-hour while he waited for Kuchinski to finish talking with Kazmaryck. Kuchinski waved Rep into his office as soon as the reception door closed behind Q.

"Is this the only disk you have from Jurimetrics?" Rep asked, returning the plastic case to Kuchinski.

"Yep."

"Have you looked at it?"

"Nope. I don't do things I don't want to do unless I get paid for it. The left-coasters were lead counsel, so I let them kill a Saturday watching the mock jury stuff. I'd found Angstrom and gotten him to dig up three students, and I figured I'd done my bit. I spent that Saturday playing golf."

"You should take a peek."

"Why? "

"Because your co-counsel are holding out on you."

"Are they now? Those rascals. What makes you say that? "

Rep told him. Kuchinski spent ten poker-faced seconds digesting the information.

"Well," he said then, "we will just by-God *see* about that."

He picked up the phone. Rep took the hint and left.

Chapter Twenty-one

"Jesus, watch what you're doing with that whip!"

"Sorry."

"We're short-handed as it is!"

"I'm a little too into it, I guess."

A man in his late twenties or early thirties, dressed in a coarse white tunic and sandals, sheepishly gathered up three intertwined lengths of dark yellow rope. He had an impressive dark brown beard, and you had to get pretty close to tell that his matching shoulder-length hair was a wig. If you did get that close you might have noticed blue eyes and other facial features that looked a bit Aryan for a first-century A.D. Jew.

"Okay," said the younger man in gray hoodie and sweatpants who had admonished the whip-wielding actor playing Jesus, "let's get set up and make this one count! It's getting cold in here!"

Melissa shivered in agreement. Four walls sheltered the stone-floored assembly area, but the Romanesque arches looking out on the cloister walk were open and let in plenty of brisk winter air. They pretty much had to be open, of course, because no one would associate Thermopane with the Temple in Jerusalem under Roman rule.

The guy in the hoodie fussed with a digital video camera on a tripod. A dozen people took their places at small wooden tables forming a rough U in front of the arches. Coins heaped in mounds, paper dollars and euros overflowing wicker baskets, and carelessly strewn stock certificates covered the tables. Balance scales and papier mâché doves in crude wooden cages completed the array of props.

The people behind the tables continued the theme of deliberate anachronism. Three were dressed in the same type of Mediterranean garb as the Jesus actor, but four were in business suits sharper than any Rep owned, two were women in long skirts and blouses, and three were in Catholic clerical garb—a monsignor, a cardinal, and a pope, Melissa thought.

The guy in the hoodie motioned to a coed, who awkwardly squatted to look at the flip-out screen on the video camera while she fingered the controls. Moving well away from her, he raised a still camera and spoke.

"Pan slowly along the tables….Slooowwwly….No hurry…. Zoom in on the money….Again, get each kind….Now pull back steady to wide angle….And…and…Jesus, go!"

The Jesus actor unfurled his whip of cords and snapped it over his head. He strode menacingly forward, lashed the floor, then raised the whip again and swished it in a vicious-looking, arm's-length parabola. His hair flew behind him and his muscular body stretched athletically as he drew the whip back again in terrifying preparation for another lash. The money-changers scattered in entirely plausible panic. Tables clattered against the uneven stone as fleeing brokers upset them. Coins spilled noisily on the floor. Currency flung into the air swirled like confetti.

"Perfect! " the guy in the hoodie yelled. "Cut! "

Jesus angrily threw over a couple of tables that were still standing. He whirled right and left, as if he hadn't had quite gotten the flogging out of his system.

"Got it!" the director yelled.

The whip swished through the air and mangled a euro floating around waist level.

"Enough with the bloody whip, dammit!" the director shrieked. "Chill, Jesus! Down boy!"

The actor playing Jesus froze and then sagged, as if reacting to a sudden drop in adrenaline. Three of the money-changers hurried up to him with congratulations and a parka. The one in papal gear, however, skirted the scene and found his way to Melissa. He doffed his tiara on the way, collapsed it, and stuck the now flat headgear under his left arm.

"Greg Huebner," he said, holding his right hand out to Melissa.

"Good afternoon, father. Or should I say your Holiness?"

"I figured it was my only shot."

"Were you just supposed to be a generic pontiff, or one of the popes in particular?"

"Leo the Tenth," Huebner said. "The one who authorized the sale of indulgences that made Martin Luther so cross. Digital magic will put a recognizable face on as many of the money-changers as we can: Jim Baker of PTL fame, Jimmy Swygert, Aimee Semple McPherson *et cetera*. We're striving for ecumenical abuse. The title is *Matthew 21:12-13.*"

"I couldn't have quoted chapter and verse but I picked up the allusion," Melissa said. "Will this be a movie or a still picture?"

"Both. Forty-two seconds on Youtube as part of a subtly manipulative youth ministry recruiting campaign, and a mural for our food pantry."

"I'm surprised you're not a little shy about calling the youth thing 'subtly manipulative.'"

"We have it on good authority that we should be as cunning as serpents. Now, I understand from Tereska that we might have a stray sheep thinking about returning to the fold."

"I'm afraid it's a little more complicated than that. Your cunning-as-serpents line is oddly apropos."

"Perhaps you'd better explain."

She did. Huebner listened in thoughtful silence but with growing and obvious consternation.

"So you think she has information about Professor Angstrom's murder, and you want to get if from her yourself instead of just turning her over the mercies of the cops."

"Right."

"And because she's a very hard-shelled young woman, you've come up with a story about coming back to the Church in order to gain her confidence. Are you hoping that I'll add some instant credibility to your pose?"

"I may be an apostate but I'm not a moral cretin. I feel bad enough about deceiving a vulnerable young woman without asking a priest to collaborate with me."

"I hope you do find your way back. " Huebner flashed a nimble, quicksilver smile. "We could use a little bracing moral certitude. But if you're not looking for collaboration, what *do* you want from me?"

"I want your advice on how to reach her."

"How sure are you that she's the one who trapped you in the stairwell?"

"As sure as you are about the existence of Purgatory. When I mildly alluded to the incident on Friday she blushed like a scolded sixth-grader."

"A burglary and a murder with the same victim," Huebner mused, "and a possible cover-up of the burglary. I suppose they *could* be unrelated—just as randomly colliding electrons *could* have accidentally formed the spectacularly intricate and miraculously fascinating world around us. But a prudent man wouldn't bet on it, would he?"

"Once a Thomist, always a Thomist."

"Sorry, couldn't resist. But if you want to know about Tereska you might start with her name."

"It's Polish, obviously."

"But it's not the version her mother picked. Her baptismal certificate has the American version: 'Teresa.' She adopted the Polish spelling in high school, in honor of Pope John Paul the Second, the Polish pope."

"I knew she was fervent, but I didn't know she'd taken it quite that far."

"It goes beyond fervor with Tereska. Closer to obsession. Do you know her email address?"

"No. I vaguely recall something offbeat from when she took one of my classes last year, but I can't remember it."

"'Outofatube@hotmail.com'"

"Sounds like a heavy metal group."

"Tereska was conceived by artificial insemination. Thinking she has a hypodermic for a father has left an emotional gap in her life. She hasn't *lost* a parent; as she sees it, one of her parents mysteriously just *wasn't there. Ever.*"

"Perhaps subconsciously she's been looking for a father-substitute," Melissa suggested.

"Right. Like John Paul the Second. Or even the Church itself."

"Or Professor Angstrom."

"That thought had crossed my mind," Huebner said. "But I'd rather leave the dime-store psychology to people with the credentials for it."

"So where does that leave us?"

"If you're going to reach Tereska you'll have to do it at the emotional level. Pascal was right: the heart has its reasons that the mind cannot grasp. Tereska is brainy enough to parse syllogisms with a Jesuit, but on this she'll have to know with her heart before she can accept with her intellect."

"Would you be willing to talk to her? She admires you very much."

"And I admire Stephen Hawking. But when he says something that I know in my soul is wrong I shrug him off like a high school junior who thinks he's a philosopher because he's read three chapters of Nietzsche."

"Do you have any suggestions, then?"

"Trust yourself. Your instincts seem solid and you're on the side of the angels. Go with what feels right at the moment."

"You mean call her and keep lying to her?" Melissa demanded.

"It's easier to sell bread to a hungry man. Wait for her to call you. And as for lying—well, be cunning as a serpent. I know it won't be pleasant, but you've started down that road and now there's no other way."

"As understatements go, 'won't be pleasant' is inspired. I'm not used to self-reproach. If I were a believer I'd say God is testing me."

"Fortunately, God grades on a curve."

"That doesn't make it any easier."

"Hey, if this were easy a Presbyterian could handle it."

"A little partisan humor?" Melissa chuckled in spite of herself.

"Why not? Thomas More joked on the scaffold. Your situation isn't as grim as his. Just be careful about your holy lie."

"I know. I might trip myself up."

"Not only that," the priest said, eyes twinkling slyly. "You might start to believe it."

Chapter Twenty-two

"Where will you be bar-hopping later on?" Rep asked Kuchinski as he poured Moët-Hennessey into three glasses. "Water Street or Brady Street?"

"Neither, thank you very much. New Year's Eve is like Saint Patrick's Day: Amateur Drunk Night. I'm a professional."

"Do you have a new trial date for Jimmy Clevenger yet?"

"Scheduling conference week after next. I'd bet on late March. I'm *really* hoping I can figure out what Angstrom was planning on selling to Jimmy's mom before he went to his eternal reward."

"Any progress on that front?" Melissa asked.

"Not much. Whoever iced him took his computer, his briefcase, and his Blackberry—so they definitely didn't want mom to have whatever it was."

"Well," Melissa said, "the tease that he sent to Valerie Clevenger was Finnegan's letter closing the Goettinger investigation. She represented the company, so she must know most of the details. Could Angstrom have known something she didn't that could hurt the case against Jimmy?"

"Sure," Kuchinski said. "Just as a wild guess, something about how maybe the investigation shouldn't have been dropped and about why it was anyway. He could have picked it up researching that corporate history. But that doesn't tell us what the dirty linen was."

"You two barristers are going to have to help the absent-minded professor out on this one. Suppose Angstrom could prove that Finnegan handled the Goettinger matter incompetently or even corruptly. Why would that be a defense for Jimmy? He either threatened Carolyn Hoeckstra or he didn't. What does Finnegan's integrity have to do with that?"

"That's an excellent question," Rep said.

"And it doesn't have a pretty answer," Kuchinski said. "What it comes down to is the way juries decide cases."

"Explain," Melissa said, realizing a bit late that she sounded like she was addressing an undergraduate who'd said something flippant about Yeats.

"In a criminal case, the government starts off wearing a big white hat. The jury assumes the government attorneys are the good guys and must know something bad about the defendant, whether they can say it in court or not."

"So if the defense can somehow show that the government's hat is tattletale gray, its natural advantage evaporates and the evidence suddenly looks a little different."

"Exactly. I'm not sure that's what the barons at Runnymede had in mind when they put trial-by-jury in *Magna Carta*, but that's the way it's worked out here in the colonies."

"You're not going to try to make the jury believe that the government killed Angstrom to suppress the evidence, are you?" Melissa asked.

"I'm not that crazy. There are too many suspects that make a lot more sense—starting with Taylor Gates, who has used poison in half his thrillers."

"How would Gates being the killer work?" Rep asked. "You figure Angstrom got Amy Lee to shop his story because he had something on Gates and Gates decided to shut him up?"

"It's a theory. The mock-jury exercise gave Angstrom a story idea. There has to be some explanation for a newby hooking Amy Lee."

"Do we know if Gates was at the Notre Dame conference?"

"No idea."

"Hmm," Rep said.

"Hmm," Melissa said.

"Like I said, it's a theory."

"It'd be more fun to pin it on Mignon," Rep said. "At least we know he was in Chicago on the day of the murder."

"Without any obvious reason to be," Kuchinski said. "Except an apparently urgent desire to talk to Carolyn Hoeckstra."

"He certainly had a motive," Melissa said. "But I'm having trouble seeing him acquiring an exotic poison and forcing it into Angstrom's mouth."

"Right." Kuchinski arched an eyebrow. "Tell the Scarsdale Diet doctor how harmless you mild-mannered academics are."

"Fair point. He dumps a prep school headmistress and the next thing he knows she's using him for target practice."

"A poor example of anger management," Rep said, "but a real tribute to the quality of American marksmanship."

"As long as we're indicting people," Kuchinski said, "it would be very convenient for my client if we could pin it on Carolyn Hoeckstra. Motive, opportunity, and she's no one's candidate for Miss Congeniality."

"You really think she'd kill someone just to keep Angstrom from getting helpful information to Clevenger?" Rep asked.

"If the information made her father or his company look bad I could see her taking a dim view of anyone shopping it around, whether it hurt the case against Jimmy or not," Melissa said.

Rep glanced over at Melissa. With the rim of her champagne flute pressed against her lips she looked pensively toward the east, where the newborn year crept over the reveling city.

"Well," Kuchinski said, slapping his thighs and rising, "thanks for the hospitality. We've seen the new year in and I'd better get back home before the streets are littered with drunken ethnic stereotypes."

Rep and Melissa rose to show him out. Rep noticed that Melissa did so a bit distractedly.

"Something on your mind?" he asked as they strolled back to the couch.

"I'm thinking of the least likely suspect."

"Valerie Clevenger?" Rep's voice rose in astonishment.

"Unless I was delusional the afternoon of the murder she isn't a suspect at all. Tereska Bleifert was at the Notre Dame conference. And I got a call this afternoon from one of the Chicago detectives asking whether she had a history with Angstrom— seduced and abandoned, bad grades, that kind of thing."

"Any hints about what stimulated that provocative query?"

"Someone apparently saw her speaking with Angstrom at the conference. She seemed very intense."

"From what you've said about her I'd say she's often intense," Rep said. "Besides, I'd find it a lot easier to see her as a candidate if the killer had cut off Angstrom's testicles with a fish fillet knife. There's something treacherous and cowardly about poison that clashes with your description of her."

"Some people call poison the woman's weapon."

"That's sexist."

"That doesn't mean it's not true."

"Sounds like a reach to me. I suspect the only reason you're struggling with it is that you'd blame yourself if she did it."

Their phone rang. Melissa recognized Bleifert's number as she answered.

"Hello, Ms. Bleifert."

"Hi, Professor Pennyworth. I'm not calling too late, am I?"

"Not at all."

"I was wondering how Father Huebner worked out."

"He said that you and I should talk."

"*Us?* About, uh—"

"Yes, about that. Are you free this coming Friday?"

"I guess. I mean, I'm like, sure. Absolutely."

"How about Ma Fischer's? My treat."

"Uh, great," Bleifert stammered. "I mean, thanks."

"No, thank *you*. I'll see you at seven."

"Very artful," Rep said after Melissa hung up. "Everything you said was at least approximately true."

"Do I detect a note of reproach, beloved?"

"Hardly. After standing here without objecting, I couldn't reproach you without indicting myself. *Qui tacet consentit.*"

"That seems like the third Latin phrase I've heard out of you in the last month, and the third one I haven't understood."

"'Silence implies consent.' Your grammy Seton could probably have translated it for you."

Melissa drained her champagne flute then abruptly lowered it and looked levelly toward Rep.

"You know what? You're absolutely right."

"Don't look so surprised."

"I have a feeling that I'm going to have a busy weekend."

"After you talk to Bleifert?"

"After I talk to Bleifert and Hoeckstra, which I'd like to do before I talk to Bleifert."

"And when you said *you* were going to have a busy weekend, I take it you meant *we*."

"Two souls in one body."

"My torts professor told me to stick with English," Rep said. "I should have listened to her."

Chapter Twenty-three

The first Friday of January, 2008

"'Weight to value ratio' are the last words I remember dad saying to me," Hoeckstra said to Melissa as she nodded toward a pigeon-holed rack. "Hand me a blank from the middle hole on the bottom, willya?"

"Do you mean this metal bar?" Melissa pulled a hunk of dull silver steel about two feet long and two inches square from the hole.

"Right. Virgin bar stock. Sorry for the jargon. Habit."

"Thanks for agreeing to see me."

"It was the least I could do after pissing you off last fall. I really didn't mean to. I probably should have written you a formal apology, but my mother figured she'd pretty much done the mom-thing once she got me on the pill at fifteen. She never got around to teaching me manners."

Hoeckstra was wearing black jeans and a green t-shirt with ENGINEERS DO IT TO SPEC printed in white on its front. She stood at a machine that she'd called a CNC lathe when she pointed it out to Melissa. It was one of four that dominated the basement room of a building tucked between the Walter Schroeder Library and the Allen Bradley Hall of Science on the downtown campus of the Milwaukee School of Engineering.

"What does 'CNC' stand for?" Melissa asked as Hoeckstra
fit the bar horizontally between two disks on the lathe and spun
a handle to tighten it snugly into place.

"'Computer numerically controlled.' The summer I turned
sixteen I asked dad for a job. I was thinking of something intern-
ish, like making photocopies and running errands, so I could
stalk engineer-studs on their way back from coffee breaks. Dad
told me he'd give me a job when I could cut a blank on a CNC
lathe to the specs called out by the blueprint, plus or minus
one-thousandth of a millimeter."

"Sounds pretty formidable for a sixteen-year old."

"Formidable is who dad was and what he did. Mom's favorite
chick cliché with him was, 'If I make you so miserable, why do
you stay?' She eventually pulled it once too often and he said,
'Duty is more important than happiness.' She gaped at him for
about five seconds, then burst into tears—and she never used
that line again."

Hoeckstra consulted a blueprint unrolled on a metal work
table and held down at the corners by chunks of slag. Blue lines
and numbers surrounded a geometric drawing on blue-specked,
ivory colored paper. Turning back to the lathe, she punched
numbers into a keypad on its control panel. They showed up
bright red against black on an LED screen above the pad.

"He had a journeyman machinist named Stash train me.
Gruff, monosyllabic, always had a cigarette dangling from the
corner of his mouth. I was scared of him at first. I ended up
inviting him to my wedding. Thinking back on it, I would have
been better off if he'd been the groom."

Adjusting plastic safety goggles that she'd donned, Hoeckstra
flipped a switch and put her right foot on a pedal. The lathe
hummed to life. Almost immediately a piercing, metal-on-
metal yowl split the still air, bouncing off the concrete floor
and the brightly painted cinder-block walls. Melissa reflexively
backed up as angry blue and yellow sparks shot from the steel.
A viscous, white liquid—lubricant, Melissa guessed—oozed
with almost erotic richness over the bar. With delicate hand

movements Hoeckstra gently guided the disk-assembly that turned the bar over blades whirling so fast they were invisible. Her pressure on the foot-pedal varied subtly from moment to moment. Mesmerized by the steady hum and howling crescendos of the lathe, Melissa stood in silence, all but motionless as minutes passed.

"It took me two weeks to get it done," Hoeckstra said then, her raised voice intruding abruptly on the high-pitched grinding from the lathe. "I've never been so proud of anything in my life."

"Did you land your intern job?"

"I told dad I wanted to work in the machine shop. He had to work out a deal with the union. They ginned up an apprenticeship program for me. They let me work there all summer, thirty-seven-and-a-half hours a week, but I had to have a union machinist standing right behind me every blessed minute."

"To protect you?" Melissa asked.

"To protect the seniority list. Dad had laid off eighty machinists in three years. There were dozens of guys with union cards who had more right to that job than I did. So I had to be completely redundant. The only way I could work there was if a guy with a union card was getting full pay without doing a lick of work every minute I was on the shop floor."

Without warning the searing cry from the lathe stopped. Melissa's eyes darted from Hoeckstra's face to the machine. Lines of red light shot over the metal bar, now round instead of rectangular, as laser beams measured its dimensions against the specifications Hoeckstra had programmed into the lathe. Green numbers flashed on the screen: +0.000.

"You're showing remarkable patience," Hoeckstra said, as she again examined the shop drawing. "You've been here almost fifteen minutes and I've spent the whole time showing off."

"I've watched hours of performance art without seeing anything remotely as beautiful or moving as what you just did. That was poetic."

Hoeckstra glanced over at her with a sly grin.

"You ain't seen nothin' yet."

She flipped another switch and braced her hands on a different set of controls. With a deep whir a sinister looking tube rose from behind the machine and rotated into place above the freshly rounded bar. Hoeckstra took a chuck-key and a drill bit from a tool drawer in the lathe's base, fit the bit into the chuck at the end of the tube, and tightened it with the key. When she flipped a second switch a high-speed hum greeted them. The tube descended inexorably toward the bar. Indifferent alike to the bar's howling protest and the pathetic fallacy, the drill bored relentlessly into the bar, penetrating it with a subtle admixture of finesse and brutality.

What would a nineteenth-century lyric poet have made of this if it had baptized him into the machine age the way a locomotive did Wordsworth? Melissa wondered. *Would we now have four stanzas—or twenty-four cantos—describing blue and yellow sparks as metallic blood? Would he have scandalized his Victorian audience with an offhand reference to the phallic bit drilling with controlled but pitiless violence into the virgin bar stock?*

Again the lathe stopped. The drill tube withdrew, shards of the metal it had shredded still clinging to the threads in the bit. Hoeckstra pulled a heavily padded mitten onto her right hand and removed the bar from the lathe.

"Part one-a of a Dowling rocker-arm assembly. Sixty-five dollars, FOB seller's dock."

"Very impressive."

"A journeyman machinist capable of turning out one of these every twelve minutes would earn thirty-one-seventy-five an hour. Call it thirty-two to make the math easier. Once you pay for workers' comp, unemployment compensation taxes, payroll taxes, and health benefits, the total labor burden for someone making that much is forty-eight dollars an hour—and that's just for labor. You haven't paid for the bar stock or the machine or the light bill or the rent yet, not to mention carrying charges for inventory or interest on your line of credit or little extras like lawyers, accountants, and payroll clerks."

"It sounds like you could lose money pretty easily."

"You could, but that's capitalism. The problem is China. Total labor burden for a machinist at a Chinese factory is less than eight dollars an hour U.S. And if some tree-hugger over there whines about how the slag runoff is hurting the fishies, the factory managers don't call their lawyers. They just kick the tree-hugger's ass into the nearest river."

"So how can a factory like Goettinger survive?"

"Two ways. One: re-invent itself as a specialty job-shop. Eight machinists instead of a hundred-twenty. Special order, quick delivery stuff. Onesies and twosies. Custom work. Two: weight-to-value ratio."

"What's that?"

"You make really heavy stuff—stuff that has a high weight and volume relative to its cost. A concrete casting with a four-meter radius, for example. You can't make that in China and ship it here, even if you use slave labor. It doesn't cost enough to cover the freight and material charges. The day before he died, dad was working on ways to apply that principle to machine tools."

Hoeckstra laid the bar lovingly in a bin at the end of the lathe and pulled off her mitten.

"I'll clean this up later. Let's go into the little sanctuary that MSOE provides to thank me for all the money dad gave it."

Hoeckstra led Melissa toward a small, darkened office in the far corner of the basement. A white-on-black embossed plate on the door said:

HOECKSTRA
PRIVATE

As soon as she was inside the office and had clicked on its fluorescent lights, Hoeckstra lifted the tail of her t-shirt to mop perspiration from her face. This exposed a midriff as taut and sleek as any model's. Melissa noticed a faint but unmistakable odor of burned pipe tobacco.

"Something to drink?" Hoeckstra asked, circling to the other side of a gray and silver metal desk.

"Water is fine."

"Can do."

Hoeckstra took a shot glass out of the top right-hand drawer of her desk, set it on the surface, and pulled a small plastic bottle of Aqua Vita and a pint of Jim Beam from the bottom drawer. She filled the shot glass with whiskey, then handed the bottled water to Melissa. As Melissa took it, Hoeckstra's fingers brushed hers, lingering for an insinuating half-second before breaking away.

"I noticed that watch you're wearing during the meeting in Li's office," Melissa said. "I'm guessing it was your father's."

"Yep. Has everything but a slide rule."

"He must have meant a great deal to you."

"He meant *everything* to me. He was what winning was to Vince Lombardi: not the main thing but the only thing."

"Just out of curiosity, were you playing head games with Bleifert when you made a big deal about her not smoking during that meeting?"

"No, I'm a real prig about it. When I was a freshman at Downer dad caught me smoking. He didn't smack me or ground me or even holler at me. He just said, 'That's either stupid or weak, and you're not stupid. I'm very disappointed in you.' Then he walked away. I've never had another cigarette."

"Did you take up meerschaums instead? Because someone has been smoking a pipe in here, and not all that long ago."

Hoeckstra took a quick pull at her shot glass and grinned. Opening the top desk drawer, she took out a briar pipe and a pouch of Sir Walter Raleigh tobacco. She began fingering tobacco parsimoniously into the pipe's bowl.

"This pipe was dad's. Once a month or so I fill it about half-full, light the pipe, and blow about six puffs around this office."

"To preserve a smell that reminds you of him."

"Right. I can just barely stand the smoking part, but the odor and the memory are worth it. Is that neurotic enough for you?"

"Proust spun eight volumes out of a mouthful of French pastry. I teach literature, so I can't begrudge you the pleasures of sensual memory."

"Fair enough. So. Why did you want to see me?"

"Because I think I might have a line on the document that was taken from Professor Angstrom's office."

"And you'd like to know if the reward offer is still good?"

"No. If I get my hands on it I'm going to try to set up a meeting where all interested parties can examine it at the same time. I wanted to know if I should include you."

"Absolutely." Hoeckstra struck a long kitchen match against the seat of her jeans and, with a frown of distaste, lit the pipe, took an unenthusiastic puff, and whiffed dark gray smoke toward the back wall of the office. "Where do you think you can dig the thing up?"

"I can't say yet. May I ask you one more thing?"

"Yep—especially if it involves slipping into something more comfortable."

"Am I kidding myself, or are you actually trying to seduce me?"

"The latter. Is it working?"

"Nope," Melissa said.

"Hmm. Maybe I've lost a step without realizing it."

"Perhaps I should just thank you for your hospitality and get going."

"Oh don't get all senior common room on me. I meant it as a compliment."

"What's your idea of an insult?"

"Are academics allowed to feel insulted by come-ons from bisexuals these days? Isn't that a badge of intolerance? Well, never mind. You could have left a voice-mail asking me about the meeting, so the next question is probably your real reason for being here. Go ahead and ask it."

"Do you blame Valerie Clevenger for your father's death?"

"Whoa. Where did that come from?"

"I've seen you in action twice. You're at least as big and strong as Jimmy Clevenger, and you've got enough attitude for him and six more like him. No way he scared you into jumping off your own boat. He couldn't do that the best day he ever had. If you'd

thought he was about to attack you wouldn't have swum for it.
You would have mopped the deck up with him."

"You weren't there. You can't know what it was like."

"Maybe. But that's where my question came from. I can't
figure out why you're wasting your time on that pathetic punk,
so I'm wondering whether your real target is his mother."

"You're totally full of it, but I'll answer your question anyway,"
Hoeckstra said. "To make up for insulting you by proposing a
little girl-on-girl. Dad had a heart condition. Atrial fibrillation
complicated by severe arrhythmia. He was taking a cocktail of
drugs to control it. You with me so far?"

"Yep."

"One of the drugs was Diltiazem. Four-hundred-eighty
milligrams a day. The EMTs found a partially full bottle in his
pocket at the scene. But the autopsy after he died didn't find a
trace of Diltiazem in his body."

"So he was forgetting to take a critical medication?"

"He wasn't *forgetting* anything. The number of pills missing
from the bottle matched the number he should have taken since
he'd last gotten the prescription filled. Besides, dad didn't forget
things like that. He had ticklers and reminders and back-ups for
everything important. He was flushing two pills a day down the
toilet."

"Why?"

"Catholic suicide. You can't kill yourself, but heroic measures
to prolong life aren't required. He stopped taking the medication
and let nature take its course."

"Yet you told me he was working on an ambitious plan to
revitalize his company," Melissa said. "That doesn't sound like
someone giving up on life."

"Exactly. Something emotionally shattering must have happened to him. Something that took everything out of him."

"The end of a love affair, for example?"

"Don't know for sure, but I really doubt it. Dad didn't make
the kind of emotional investments in people that produce tragic

gestures over a lost love. My guess is that whatever it was involved the company and was very bad."

"Criminal misconduct?" Melissa guessed. "White collar crime is Valerie Clevenger's specialty. Wasn't he consulting her about legal issues?"

"'Consulting' is an interesting word for what dad was doing with her."

"They were lovers?"

"They were sleeping together. I don't think love had much to do with it."

"They were conducting an affair while the company was sending her legal business? That's quite a coincidence."

"I don't think it was any coincidence. It wouldn't surprise me if she billed their sack-time to 'Business Development' on her daily reports."

"How far back did their tryst go?" Melissa asked.

"A while. It started just after she came up from Houston—and just before she got Goettinger Corporation as a client."

"Did it bother you while you were growing up?"

"I'd be lying if I said it didn't. But seeing Jimmy Clevenger at the funeral with Valerie ratcheted things way up. I didn't know then how long they'd been hooking up, and the thought crossed my mind that I might have a sniveling half-brother I didn't know about. That's why I looked into it further."

"Looked into it how?"

Hoeckstra dug in her desk and pulled out a spiral-bound report about two inches thick with **CONFIDENTIAL** stamped in royal blue on its buff cover.

"Kroll and Associates. One of the biggest private investigation firms in the country. Cost a mint, but it was worth it. I could tell you how many fillings she has if you wanted to know."

"What was Kroll's verdict on the half-brother issue?"

"Negative. No way they'd been doing it that long. Plus, during the entire conceptive period, as these stiffs called it, Clevenger was in Houston and dad was in China trying to sell machine tools to the commies. Turns out that Jimmy Clevenger's father is…someone else."

"Who?"

"I'm not ready to go there with you."

Melissa barely heard the words. With the precision of a CNC lathe cutting virgin bar stock, her mind picked up oddities and anomalies from the last five months and clicked them into place.

"Taylor Gates?" she asked. "Is he James *Taylor* Clevenger's father?"

"I said I'm not getting into it."

"It would explain a lot of things. Like Gates being here for the trial, and Jimmy getting a Ferrari defense even though Valerie has a Buick income."

"You can insinuate all you want. I'm not going to answer you."

"You have answered me. Were you hoping Kroll would find something to pin your father's death on Valerie?"

"I may be a neurotic, but I'm not a fantasist," Hoeckstra said, although Melissa noticed that for the first time in the conversation Hoeckstra didn't meet her eyes. "What killed dad was whatever criminal disgrace he was having Clevenger handle. When the lion hunts the jackal feeds—but that doesn't make the jackal the killer."

"And you're afraid that the material stolen from Angstrom's office would disclose whatever that criminal disgrace was," Melissa guessed.

"Bingo. The case your husband handled for Angstrom settled because Angstrom had something on the company."

"I wouldn't know about that."

"There's no other explanation. My own shyster said that without big-time dirt that case had nothing but nuisance value. The only reason to break into Angstrom's office would be to get that material, and the only reason to get it would be to use it."

Melissa thought that over for half-a-minute as Hoeckstra took another half-hearted pull on the pipe-stem and the acrid smell of burning pipe tobacco tickled her nose.

"I think you're wrong," she told Hoeckstra then. "But I'll promise you this. If I get my hands on that material, it won't be to use it—or to help anybody else use it."

"Best offer I've had all day."

"Well," Melissa shrugged as she glanced at her watch, "it's barely one o'clock in the afternoon. The day isn't over yet."

Chapter Twenty-four

"I think that the traditional lawyerly response to a suggestion like yours is something along the lines of, 'This is highly irregular,'" Li said to Melissa forty-five minutes later after she had seated herself in his office.

"Very old school. I approve. I believe your next comment is supposed to start with 'nevertheless.'"

"Nevertheless, this is a rather delicate situation."

"The murder of a tenured professor with members of the university community potentially implicated? I should say so."

"Professors come and professors go." Li shrugged. "And if I had my choice, I'd rather have people here implicated in murder than in, say, fraudulent procurement of federal grant money or fiddling the results of scientific studies."

"I guess you have to have priorities."

"The problem here is the backstory—the things Angstrom was doing that might have gotten him killed. They could compromise the university's reputation, and even worse get us screamed about gleefully by the wing-nuts on rant radio. If the Angstrom investigation is going to blow up in our face, I'd like the chancellor to hear about it from me before he reads it under Boone Fletcher's by-line. That makes your idea worth a try."

"You don't have to thank me," Melissa said. "The expression on your face is enough."

"I'll see if I can get something out between now and the end of the day."

"You won't need three hours to write an email inviting a handful of people to a meeting, will you?"

"I'll need scarcely three minutes to write the email. I'll need three hours to cover my rear end before I send it."

"I'll leave that part in your more than capable hands." Melissa rose, shook hands briefly with Li, and turned toward the door.

"Deeds and wills," Li muttered as she left his office. "I should have put out my shingle in Tomah, Wisconsin and spent my career drawing up deeds and wills for prosperous dairy farmers."

About the time the door closed behind Melissa at UWM, Rep was taking a seat in Kuchinski's office as a male voice on the speaker-phone approached the wind-up clauses in what sounded like a long sentence.

"...trial-prep stuff for the first trial is buried deep in the archives, and I certainly can't sort out one stimulus from another in my memory. Have you checked with Jurimetrics?"

"I have." Kuchinski's tone suggested just a hint of the irritation that Rep could read on his face. "They referred me to you. 'All case-related communications go through liaison counsel' were their exact words."

"Well, Walt, you know, we kind of have our hands full preparing for the second trial right now."

"I think that final mock-jury stimulus might be a real important part of our preparation."

"You may well be right about that, Walt. That's an excellent thought. I'll put that on my to-do list."

"I'd put it up there fairly high on that list, if I were you," Kuchinski said. "If you blow me off on this, the next item on your to-do list might be finding new local counsel."

"Now, Walt, don't get bent out of shape," the voice said soothingly. "I'll do everything I can, but it's the client's call. You know that."

"You may well be right about that, Henry. That's an excellent thought. And I don't know about you, but *Valerie* Clevenger ain't my client in this case."

He punched a button to break the connection.

"Do you think you'd get anywhere going directly to Jimmy?" Rep asked.

"No way. He'll do whatever mom says."

"That's when you ask for written instructions."

"Right. And asking for written instructions from your client is generally the last thing you do before you get fired."

Li clicked Confidential from the drop-down box for Status on his email window, and High from the box for Importance. He reviewed the addressees: Assistant Dean René Cyntrip Mignon; Assistant Professor Melissa Seton Pennyworth; Tereska Bleifert; Taylor Gates; and Carolyn Hoeckstra. He checked the list of those receiving copies: Dean/Non-Academic Administration; University Vice-president/Risk Management; Director/University Public Affairs; Director/University Security. Then, one last time, he reviewed the text:

Ladies and Gentlemen:

I am happy to report the possible recovery of a document purloined from Professor Angstrom's office last fall. I stress that at this time such recovery is a highly tentative possibility, not an accomplished fact, and must be treated with a great deal of discretion and finesse. I propose to discuss the matter with interested parties in my office on Wednesday at noon.

It should go without saying, but in an abundance of caution I will nevertheless say, that both the fact and the subject of the proposed meeting are highly confidential and should not be disclosed to anyone other than the addressees of this notice (and, of course, their counsel if they wish).

Regrets only.

Li

Li took a moment to congratulate himself on the parenthetical reference to counsel in the last line. He hit PRINT so that he'd have a hard copy for his own files. Then he hit SEND.

Rising from his desk, he left his office and walked approximately sixty feet to a small lounge. He filled a glass with icecubes from the freezer compartment of the refrigerator, bought a caffeine-free Diet Coke from one of the vending machines and, as he poured the cola over the ice, reflected with poignant nostalgia on past years when he was allowed to drink caffeinated beverages and eat red meat. Drink poured and sipped, he picked up a copy of the *Milwaukee Journal Sentinel* from the counter, discarded the Metro, Sports, and Business sections, and briskly read the comics.

Then he returned to his office. As he put the can and glass on separate leather and brass coasters, he glanced at his watch: 4:47. Twelve minutes since he'd hit SEND.

His phone rang. He answered.

"Boone Fletcher, *Journal Sentinel*," the voice said. "So what's the deal with this meeting next week?"

"No comment," Li said, and hung up.

He took another sip of caffeine-free Diet Coke and smiled. He had bet himself that it would take less than twenty minutes for his email to be leaked to Fletcher, and he enjoyed winning.

Chapter Twenty-five

"Smoking or non-smoking?"

"Your call," Melissa told Bleifert.

"Non-smoking," the young woman said firmly.

The hostess led them to a booth on the far side of Ma Fischer's, a diner-style restaurant about half-way between UWM and downtown Milwaukee. Bleifert began speaking even as she slid in on her side of the booth.

"I don't understand why Father Huebner suggested that you talk to me. I'm no good on the usual hang-ups non-believers have about Catholicism."

"I don't think he was really focusing on—"

"I mean, like, about two weeks ago McHunk says, 'Okay, what about Opus Dei?' And I'm, like, forget it, you know? I mean, I know *The Da Vinci Code* was just making stuff up, and I understand intellectually where Opus Dei is coming from, but I just don't connect with it."

"The details were never what hung me up," Melissa said.

"Then what did?"

"The big picture."

A waitress came with bread and ice-water. She took out her pad and looked at them hopefully.

"What's good?" Melissa asked.

"Brat *mitt*," the waitress said.

"That's Milwaukeean for bratwurst with sauerkraut," Bleifert explained in response to Melissa's quizzical look. "I'll have that."

"For two," Melissa said.

"Nice call on the non-smoking section, by the way," Melissa said as the waitress padded off. "A guy who walked in right behind us asked for smoking and he's still waiting for a table."

"So, big picture. I'm not sure where to start."

"Start with yourself. You're passionate about the Church. Why?"

She didn't have to ask twice. The seemingly innocent question triggered a monologue as intense in its way as Hoeckstra's lathe demonstration that afternoon. It began a nanosecond after the Big Bang and before it ended on the Fields of Armageddon the guy Melissa had pointed out sat serenely in the smoking section and bread, salad, and entrées had found their way to Melissa and Bleifert. As she noticed Melissa slice delicately into her bratwurst, Bleifert seemed to sense that she should wrap things up.

"What it comes down to, I guess, is what if it's true? I mean, maybe it isn't, but what if it is? If it's true, the incarnation is the most *consequential* thing that ever happened. If it's true, everything *means* something. When I have doubts—and I have a lot of them, often—I think, how can I turn my back on the most exciting thing there could ever be, just because maybe it's not there? How could I risk not being part of it?"

"Wow, to coin a phrase."

"I guess I'd better eat something," Bleifert said a bit sheepishly. "I really turned into a motor-mouth, didn't I?"

"You did what I asked you to do. But you're right—you'd better eat."

The sheer, glowing joy that radiated from Bleifert made the guilt shrouding Melissa seem all the more leaden. Bleifert was thrilled at the thought of Melissa *coming back*, rejoining Bleifert and roughly a billion others on the great, transcendent arc of History with a capital H. Melissa's gray lie now seemed stygian black. When she eventually confessed it, Bleifert would be shattered. When the time came to make that confession, Melissa had no idea how she'd even start.

"Listen, professor," Bleifert said after a mouthful of bratwurst, "there's something I've got to tell you."

"Oh?"

"Yeah. I mean, I feel like a hypocrite sitting here like this saint guiding you back to the one true faith and all that stuff when, ah, er—"

"When what?" Melissa made the prompt as gentle as she could.

"Okay. I, uh, I guess I wasn't completely truthful with you when you asked me about the night of the break-in. The scream and everything."

"That was you?"

"That was me. I mean 'I.' That was I."

"Good catch."

"I was outside Mignon's office, trying to get in. I heard someone coming. I thought it was Mignon. I mean, who else would be coming up there at that time of night?"

"Who indeed?"

"I wanted to divert his attention, draw him away from the area, and hang him up for a few minutes."

"To give you a chance to cover your tracks."

"Yeah."

"The idea of your escapade being to find something in Mignon's office."

"Right."

"Specifically, to find the original of the papal document that you thought Mignon might have stolen from Professor Angstrom's office."

Bleifert's head snapped up and surprise washed the blush away from her candid features.

"No. I wasn't afraid he'd taken that. I mean, that wouldn't do him any good, would it? He couldn't use it without exposing himself as a thief."

"But he could keep Professor Angstrom from using it. Both out of spite and because it undermines his condemnation of Pius the Twelfth."

"No way." Bleifert shook her head emphatically. "A document like that would be a bonanza for UWM. He wouldn't pass up that kind of opportunity. He'd just say his thinking on Pius had 'evolved' and his previous views had been misinterpreted. Then he'd find some way to cut himself in on the action."

"There is nothing so bracing as the cynicism of the ingenuous." Melissa muttered this under her breath, but not as far under as she thought.

"That's good," Bleifert said, her eyes brightening with delight. "Who said that?"

"I did. Just now."

"Props for the prof!" Bleifert tendered a high fist across the table. Melissa gamely dropped her knife and touched knuckles with the coed.

"On reflection, I think you must be right about Mignon," Melissa said then. "Your analysis fits in with the overture he made to me. But if it wasn't the papal document, what were you afraid he had taken?"

Bleifert's head dropped and she rolled hooded eyes up to send a half-ashamed/half-defiant glare at Melissa.

"I'm sorry," she said in a voice devoid of contrition. "I can't tell you that."

Melissa nodded and looked idly to her right as she contemplatively chewed spiced sausage and sauerkraut. It took her about five seconds to be sure she was right.

"Okay, Tereska, here's where it is. We're talking about a murder, and it has to be related somehow to the break-in."

"You're not suggesting that I killed Professor Angstrom, are you? I loved him like a father, even though I had to brush off a proposition now and then."

Loved him like a father—paging Dr. Freud.

"Of course I'm not suggesting that. What I'm saying is that someone is playing hardball. I don't know who. But a guy came into this restaurant right behind us. He spent ten minutes waiting for a table in the smoking section. He has finished a cheeseburger and he's been nursing a second cup of coffee for at least five minutes—and he still hasn't smoked."

"So what?"

"So he had a reason other than cigarettes to ask for the smoking section."

"Like what?"

"On a wild guess, he wanted a seat where he could see both us and my car in the parking lot."

"Why?"

"Well, that vantage point would come in handy if a buddy of his were messing with my car and this guy wanted to make sure of warning him in case we headed off before he thought we would."

"I, uh—whoa."

"So I'm having trouble with your not telling me what you thought Mignon was after. Protecting friends is admirable, but if more lives may be in danger you have to make tough choices."

Bleifert shrank in her seat. She shook her head in a way that suggested both stubborn challenge and despair.

"Maybe I can get by without it," Melissa said musingly. "You've probably already gotten the email about a meeting in Li's office next week. I know Mignon broke into Angstrom's office and took *something*. When I accuse him at that meeting, he'll probably justify himself by saying what it was."

"No!" Bleifert snapped. "You can't do that."

"What's going to stop me?"

"I mean you mustn't do that. Because it isn't true. Mignon wasn't the one who did the break-in."

"How do you know?"

Bleifert gulped air and then took a quick swig of water. She looked like she might be about to cry. Melissa shriveled inside in a spasm of self-disgust.

"I saw him come back," Bleifert said, her voice now very soft. "Mignon. He used the faculty entrance, and I could see it from the stairwell where I was hiding. That was after the break-in had already happened."

"Fair enough. Taking Mignon off the hook, though, makes my question that much more urgent. He's the least scary suspect in the scenario. If it's someone else, the danger is greater."

"I can't take a chance on betraying Professor Angstrom," Bleifert said miserably. "Even by accident."

"Betrayal is something I can promise to avoid." Reaching across the table, Melissa took Bleifert's right hand in hers. "If what you tell me doesn't suggest a physical threat to someone else, I won't repeat it unless you and I agree that I should. I can't offer you the seal of the confessional. I won't put my hand on the Bible. I won't swear by the Blessed Virgin or by all that's holy. But I will give you my word."

Bleifert relaxed a little as she grinned in recognition.

"Chesterton, right?"

"Yes, and pretty obscure Chesterton at that. I'm impressed."

"I only had three dates in high school," Bleifert said, flippantly tossing her hair. "I had plenty of time to read."

"Professor Angstrom and Dean Mignon," Melissa said then.

"Okay." Bleifert took a deep breath, expelled it, and looked for a moment as if she were re-thinking the whole stop-smoking business. "Uh, you know Professor Angstrom had some sidelines in addition to his work at the University, right?"

"That doesn't come as a complete surprise."

"Well, technically, he's not supposed to use any university resources for that kind of thing."

"Right. We can sleep with our students, but when it comes to money we're supposed to be purer than the Vestal Virgins."

"Professor Angstrom wasn't particularly virginal in this respect. I kept a separate file for him with hard copies of expense records on his sideline projects. He needed them for taxes. That file was the first thing I looked for when I saw that his office had been broken into. It was missing."

"You were afraid Mignon had taken it so that he could retaliate against Angstrom for humiliating him at the Brontë conference?"

"Right. Mignon could have used those records to get Professor Angstrom in a lot of trouble. Maybe even get him fired."

"Tereska, it means a lot to me that you've trusted me with this. But if you want Professor Angstrom's killer to be caught, you're going to have to tell me one more thing."

"Namely?"

"What did you tell McHunk during the jury deliberations about the sex-or-swim case?"

"WHATTT?"

Melissa could tell that Bleifert was doing her level best to feign astonished indignation. She didn't come close to bringing it off.

"Professor Angstrom rounded up some UWM students for the mock-jury exercise that a jury consulting firm did in preparation for the first trial," Melissa said. "He kept some of the information from that exercise—because he thought it would come in handy in one of his sidelines, I suspect. You saw it. The jury analysis predicted a defense verdict based on certain information. For some reason that I can't figure out, the defense lawyers chose not to use all of it. The real sex-or-swim jury was warned not to discuss the case, but it wasn't sequestered. The most logical reason for Grady Schoenfeld becoming the only holdout on the panel is that he had the information the mock-jury heard but the other real jurors didn't. And the most logical explanation for that is that you told him. How am I doing?"

"Please don't get him in trouble. It was my fault."

"I'll do everything I can to keep you both out of trouble. But I gather that my theory is at least in the ballpark."

"Yeah. You're right about all that. What you said."

"'All that' is the easy part. That was just putting two and two together, with a lucky guess or two thrown in. But I still don't know what the information itself was."

Bleifert studied her plate intently, though without any apparent appetite. Then she looked up.

"I'm not going to say no, but I'm not sure I can tell you, either. I need to think this through. Can you give me through the weekend?"

"I left my thumbscrews at the office, so I guess I'll have to."

"Okay. Sunday night. Or Monday at the latest. One way or the other. I promise."

"Fair enough," Melissa said. "By the way, I enjoy hearing you talk about God. Do you feel like some coffee?"

"Sure."

Bleifert's appetite had clearly returned. By the time they'd finished their coffee she had also polished off the last of her brat *mitt*. Melissa paid the check and they left, walking past the booth of a guy who still wasn't smoking.

Melissa found her car snugly locked and apparently unmolested. She saw no scratches on the lock or on the window near the seal. When she slipped behind the wheel she didn't notice any unfamiliar hairs or stray tufts of fabric, nor any unexplained smudges on the rear-view mirror. No hints of cologne that Rep didn't use or other foreign odors. She couldn't find any evidence at all, in fact, to support her feeling that some indefinable something was slightly off.

She wondered if the theory about the non-smoker in Ma Fischer's being a lookout that she'd pitched to Bleifert was so clever that she'd ended up believing it herself; or if it was actually true, and whoever had searched her car was good enough not to leave any trace of his intrusion behind.

Or her intrusion, Melissa reminded herself.

Chapter Twenty-six

The first Saturday in January, 2008

Tereska Bleifert sat in a pew toward the back on the right side of the main aisle at St. Josephats Basilica. On the first Saturday of Lent in 2005 she had come here for confession. Looking to her left, beyond the pews on the other side of the aisle, she could see the door of the reconciliation room where Father Huebner had heard her confession.

Reconciliation room, not confessional. No booths, no grill, no kneeler, no screen. Just a couple of chairs facing each other in a room about the size of a small office. A real confessional, the old fashioned kind, stood to her right, across the side aisle that ran past the pew where she sat now. This one had a center booth for the priest, and a booth on either side of it for penitents. Each booth was smaller than the hall closet in the home she shared with her mother eight blocks away. Just enough room for the penitent to kneel in darkness and wait for the priest to slide up the cover over the grill separating the two compartments, so that in dim anonymity the age-old formula could begin: *Bless me, father, for I have sinned.*

They hadn't been using the confessional that day. Later in Lent, she knew, they would be. People would be lined up on both sides, anxious to be shriven before Easter so that they could receive communion with a clear conscience. As soon as the penitent in one booth had finished and the cover had shut and he or she had come out, the next person in line on that side would go in, kneel, wait for the priest to finish with the confession in the other booth and open the cover again on this side. They would be using that confessional and the reconciliation room and improvised stations in corners here and there around the church.

Not on the first Saturday of Lent, though. That early, the reconciliation room was ample for the handful of people seeking absolution.

"When I examined my conscience I found the pickings pretty slim." That was the way she'd started with Huebner in the reconciliation room. "My chastity is protected by lack of opportunity, so I don't have any sins against the sixth and ninth commandments, as the Church bashfully calls them. Two or three cigarettes a day won't pass for gluttony. I'm almost seventeen so they probably don't even count as disobedience. Idolatry seems like an interesting sin, but I'm having enough trouble believing in one God."

"How about something venial, just to get the ball rolling? Sneaking off to a kegger after you've told mom you're going to a friend's house to study? Swiping a Miller Lite from the 'fridge?"

"In nearly seventeen years on this planet—close to eighteen if life begins at conception—I've never done anything remotely as interesting as that."

"Yet you're here and you've come for a reason. What is it?"

"Because no one my age does. I'm the resist-peer-pressure poster girl. I'd look down on my inferiors if I had any but I don't. So I go to confession instead."

"You don't think much of your peers?"

"If there's a heaven I hope it's better than an afternoon at the mall, which is their idea of paradise. I don't know who's violating the sixth and ninth commandments with whom on *The OC* or *Laguna Beach*. Paging through *People* isn't my idea of reading. It's more like they don't think much of me. Or they wouldn't if they thought about anything. Maybe that sounds like envy."

"No, it sounds like pride. Like you blow off your classmates to let yourself off the hook. If they're not worth the effort it doesn't hurt as much when they don't like you. Saying no one is inferior to you is your clever way of saying everyone is."

"Pride in my own humility? Didn't Saint Teresa of Avila whip herself for that?"

"I'm hearing your confession, not Saint Teresa's. For your penance, I want you to spend five minutes out there thanking God for the quick tongue and the nimble wit he gave you. And if God says, 'You know what? Maybe I did something right with some other people too'—think about that."

And so she had done what he said on that Lenten Saturday almost three years ago. Said her Act of Contrition, accepted absolution, thanked the priest, and gone out to find a pew where she could say a prayer against self-pity. She had been praying in the same pew where she was now when the old guy had caught her eye.

Not all that old, really. Late fifties, she thought, but moving like someone fifteen years older. He wore a burnt orange polo shirt, mismatched with a tweed suit coat and pants. Not scruffy or seedy, like a homeless wino dressed by the Salvation Army, but looking disoriented.

He'd slipped into the south booth of the confessional that wasn't in use that day. She remembered shrugging, assuming that he'd figure out soon enough that there wasn't any priest to open the cover and listen to his sins through the grill, no absolution to be had in that old-fashioned vestige of the Catholicism he'd known growing up. She had closed her eyes tightly and prayed. *What if God answers me? What if he doesn't?*

She hadn't known if it was God talking, but less than two minutes into the prayer her conscience had prodded her, if a sharp rowel to the gut can be called a prod. The light was still on over the booth the elderly gent had entered, and by now he should have realized his mistake and emerged. Maybe he had early Alzheimers, maybe he was kneeling there confused and terrified in the dark. Rising and picking her way awkwardly along the pew, she had headed for the confessional.

Still twenty feet away, she had stopped when she saw the door open. The guy was coming out after all.

Except it wasn't the guy. The one who'd stepped through the doorway was a well-dressed woman, cradling an aqua colored file folder in her left arm. She was tall and, by Midwest standards, slender. The kind of scarf Catholic women wore to church in the 1950s covered her hair and hid most of her face. She had left the door ajar and hustled toward the vestibule.

Bleifert had hurried over and pulled the booth's door all the way open. She had seen the man's body crumpled in the rear corner, death deforming his kneeling posture into a grotesque squat, face twisted in agony, shocks of scraggly white hair falling in disorder over his forehead. The next day's *Milwaukee Journal Sentinel* would identify him as Timothy Goettinger, CEO and principal shareholder of Goettinger Corporation.

Bleifert recalled sprinting for the back of the church, pulling her cell-phone out and punching in 9-1-1 as she'd looked for the woman in the scarf. She hadn't see a sign of her in the vestibule or the parking lot, and when the 9-1-1 responder came on she'd stopped looking and concentrated on telling him to get an ambulance to St. Jo's in a big damn hurry. She told the police later about the woman, of course, but the glimpse she'd gotten left her with scant material for description and anyway, the young cop's expression said, so what? The med-techs said it was a heart attack. No wounds, no blood, no weapon. The old ticker just stopped. Besides, Bleifert's was the second 9-1-1 call. The first had probably come from the woman, who wanted to help but didn't want to kill her afternoon answering questions.

While waiting for the cops and the EMTs that afternoon, Bleifer had prayed. She would eventually get back to her interrupted penance, but before that she'd said a different prayer, for a man she didn't know, to a God she doubted, in words taught her by a Church she mocked.

Now, not quite three years later, she looked at the confessional again, dark and unused as it had been that day. She wondered what it would be like if God ever talked to her. A deep, rumbling voice in the thunder? No, she didn't think so, somehow. Maybe it was just a comfortable feeling, a growing sense of calm, a moment of clarity. Maybe that's all it was, the serene conviction from somewhere that somehow she had the right answer.

Whatever. That'll do.

"*Il Gattopardo* by Giuseppi Tomasi di Lampedusa, as instructed," Rep said as he returned to Melissa's Curtin Hall office around one o'clock on Saturday afternoon. "The coed at the checkout desk was completely unimpressed."

"You should have said '*ciao.*'" Melissa kept her eyes focused on her computer screen.

"I did. Got me nowhere. Apparently guys who read classic novels in foreign languages are a dime a dozen around here. Are you about ready to go?"

"I have one more thing to print off and then we can head home."

Melissa slipped what looked like a very old academic monograph into a manila folder. It was folded over to its sixth page, where vivid yellow highlighting emphasized a footnote. After fussing with her computer for a few seconds she looked up at Rep.

"There's a printer at the work station around the corner just down the hall from my door," she said. "One of the shelves above it is labeled 'second page letter bond.' Could you stick about eight of those pages into the printer?"

"You must have me confused with a patent lawyer. They're supposed to be good at mechanical stuff. But I'll do my best."

He managed the chore with only a paper cut or two to betray his inexperience. Then he yelled to Melissa that she could print. Ten seconds later the first page of bond rolled out of the printer. Except for an elaborate decoration at the top, it was blank. When he had all eight pages, he brought them to her. She put them into the folder with the monograph, then worked the folder, the book Rep had brought, and a paperback copy of *The Leopard* into a canvas carry-all.

"Is that the Vatican seal?" he asked.

"You got it. Papal tiara and crossed keys. All things are possible with God, according to Sister Carmelita at Saint Teresa's Academy, and most of them are accessible through Google."

"What was that thing you stuck into your briefcase just before I went to the printer?"

"An article by Professor Angstrom, very early in his career, about the emergence of proletarian consciousness in the Italian working class community in Milwaukee after the first World War. Did you know that Milwaukee's Italian community had its own newspaper?"

"That datum had escaped my attention."

"Printed in Italian, of course."

"Well, it might have created the wrong impression if they'd printed it in Swedish."

"Professor Angstrom quotes some excerpts in his article."

"In the original?"

"In the original," Melissa confirmed. "'Translation by the author.'"

"That rascal. He was just kidding when he had Bleifert tell you he needed a translator."

"Now we can go. Your only assigned task for the rest of the day will be to keep coffee coming."

"What will you be doing?"

"Practicing penmanship."

"Are you going to tell me what you're up to, or is it better that I not know?"

"*Qui tacet consentit.*"

When they got back to the building that housed their condo, a guy at a desk in the lobby (who would have been called a concierge in New York but in Milwaukee was called a guy at a desk in the lobby) handed Melissa a brown paper envelope. She recognized Bleifert's handwriting when she read her name and the words PRIVATE and CONFIDENTIAL.

She waited until they had closed the front door of their unit before she opened it. With Rep looking over her shoulder, it took her a full minute to absorb the single page of text inside:

JURIMETRICS—CLEVENGER/U.S. v.
STIMULUS VI

Assume the following facts are true, in addition to everything else you have heard.

One: In the last five years, the prosecuting attorney in this case has brought eleven cases against companies that were represented by the defendant's mother.

Two: Between three and four years ago, the prosecuting attorney considered charges against a company owned by the complaining witness—the woman who has accused the defendant of rape.

Three: Charges in that case were never brought.

What effect would these facts have on your deliberations?

"Isn't that interesting?" Rep commented. "I guess Walt can stop browbeating his co-counsel out on the West Coast."

He glanced at Melissa for confirmation. She was frowning as she pulled a flyer and a paperback book from the envelope.

"Those don't look like they're from Jurimetrics."

"They aren't. The book is *Orthodoxy: The Romance of Faith*, by Chesteron. The flyer is about a Catholic retreat for women in a couple of months. Ms. Bleifert is calling my bluff."

Chapter Twenty-seven

The first Wednesday in January, 2008

Taylor Gates didn't show up for the meeting in Li's office. He had a good excuse: the email address Li had typed in for Gates was one Li made up, and it had baffled his server. He had ignored the server's curt notification that the missive was undeliverable to that address.

Everyone else arrived punctually. As they arranged themselves around Li's desk, Melissa figured that all they needed was Nero Wolf in a yellow leather chair.

"Good afternoon," Li said. "Thank you for coming."

He took a fountain pen cased in rich lapis lazuli from the upper right-hand pocket of his vest. He didn't uncap the pen, as he apparently had no intention of writing anything. Melissa suspected that he just wanted a prop.

"Being a lawyer," Li continued, "I will begin by telling you what you already know but in language sufficiently arcane to justify nineteen years of formal education. Someone ransacked Professor Angstrom's office last fall, something over two months before his murder. One or more documents of potential scholarly, historical, and/or legal significance are missing. The perpetrator of the break-in presumably took it or them. While we have no direct evidence linking the break-in to Professor Angstrom's murder, it's hard to believe that the two incidents are unrelated.

If an outsider committed the break-in, he or she managed to get into Curtin Hall without being noticed at the guard station for the only public entrance. This suggests that the perpetrator was either an insider himself or working with one."

"You're right," Mignon growled, as if Li were a graduate student whose term paper cited only secondary sources. "Nothing new so far."

"The new element is that Professor Pennyworth may have recovered the stolen document."

"How did you bring that about, professor?" Mignon asked, looking pointedly at Melissa. "And does it by any chance have anything to do with our missing invitee?"

"On my instructions—" Li began.

"I wasn't asking you, counselor."

"I am nevertheless answering you, dean," Li said with an I'm-a-lawyer-and-you're-not edge to his voice. "I have instructed Professor Pennyworth not to disclose either how she got her hands on the document or from whom she obtained it, pending administrative decisions about sharing this information with law enforcement authorities. Certain legal privileges that the university may choose to invoke in the future could be compromised by disclosure of such information outside of what the law inelegantly calls UWM's 'control group.'"

"What's our 'control group?'" Mignon demanded.

"All you need to know for the moment is that you aren't in it."

"May we at least see the recovered document?"

"Certainly," Melissa said.

She took a manila file folder from the canvas tote at her feet. From the folder she removed a yellowed, brittle sheet of bond, covered with fussy, back-sloping longhand and encased in a glassine paper protector. She took three strides across the room to hand it to Mignon.

Handling it fastidiously with his fingertips, he laid the document delicately in his lap while he fumbled with half-moon spectacles. Hockestra and Bleifert both got out of their chairs and huddled near Mignon's right shoulder to examine the document. As Mignon's eyes scanned the page, his lips moved silently in the challenging throes of sight-translation.

"Addressed to an OAR monastery in Breslau, Czechoslovakia," Mignon said then. "I'm not sure what 'OAR' means."

"Order of Augustinian Recollect," Bleifert said.

"Dated third June 1943. ' With burning heart we hear of myriads persecuted and indeed in peril of their very lives because of their race alone. While of course remembering them in our prayers, the extreme character of the situation requires that we go yet further. It is our fervent wish that the arms of the Church be opened to them, with all practical aid and spiritual comfort we can provide.' My word. This is a real find."

"'It is our fervent wish' is the Vatican equivalent of 'Now hear this,'" Bleifert said. "'Because of their race alone' makes this is the first documentary evidence of a direct order from the pope himself to help Jewish victims of Nazi persecution."

"If it's genuine," Mignon said as Hoeckstra shrugged and returned to her chair. "Have you had this looked at by a document examination expert?"

"No."

"It seems to me that that is the next order of business."

"No," Li said, "the next order of business, as in before anyone leaves this room, is to make sure we know everything there is to know about whether the provenance of this document could reflect negatively on the integrity of this university."

Melissa retrieved the document and, as she was walking back to her chair, offered it to Li. He shook his head and sketched a dismissive gesture with his left hand, suggesting that busy lawyers operating in the temporal realm didn't have time for spiritual mumbo-jumbo.

Melissa laid the page and its plastic holder on the left rear corner of Li's desk. This chanced to be immediately beneath the ocular lens of his telescope, which sloped up at a forty-five degree angle toward his tall window—as if inviting heaven itself to scrutinize the document. If anyone noticed that she had laid it on top of the one-hundred-eight millimeter lens cap for the telescope's objective lens, they kept that observation to themselves.

"'Provenance,'" Hoeckstra asked. "Do you mean who took the thing?"

"I mean where it came from and how it got from there to here," Li said. "Including every step of the way from Breslau to this office."

"Well," Mignon said, "we have oblique evidence about some of that, in the form of comments by Professor Angstrom before his death."

"I'm all ears," Li said.

Mignon repeated the account he had previously provided to Melissa. He hadn't quite finished when he stopped abruptly and, eyes widening, rose from his chair and pointed at the document.

"Fire!" he yelped. "That thing is burning!"

A wisp of white smoke was in fact rising from the center of the plastic protecting the document. A small, brown-edged hole appeared in the paper.

Mignon and Bleifert leaped toward the precious page. They were still two yards away when Li deftly sloshed a dollop of Evian water over the hot spot and then whisked the document to the center of his desk.

"Amazing how many problems you can solve with dihydrogen oxide," he said cheerfully. "No real harm done."

"No harm?" Mignon wailed. "You may have just ruined a historic treasure. This is a catastrophe!"

"It may not be irreparably damaged," Bleifert said. "Perhaps we should begin with a prayer."

"Jesus Christ!" Mignon snapped in exasperated fury.

"Well, that's a start," Melissa sighed.

Mignon's eyes widened again as he looked more closely at Li's desk.

"You left the lens cap off your telescope, you blithering imbecile."

"Good heavens, so I did," Li said. "That *was* careless of me."

"That's what set it on fire. It was like holding a magnifying glass directly over it. The telescope focused the sun's rays onto the paper. How could you be such an idiot?"

"Please be seated," Li said calmly.

"And I suggest that you save your imprecations for a better occasion," Melissa said. "That document wasn't stolen from Angstrom's office."

Mignon and Bleifert gaped at her as they retreated to their seats. Hoeckstra looked up in mild surprise.

"Then where did it come from?" Mignon demanded.

"From Professor Pennyworth's fertile imagination," Li said.

"It's a forgery I concocted over the weekend," Melissa explained. "I cobbled it together with words and phrases that I took from a classic Italian novel called *The Leopard*. Not quite as convincing as the Donation of Constantine, but good enough for our limited purposes."

"And what might those be?" Mignon asked.

"To prove conclusively that neither you nor Ms. Bleifert stole the missing document from Angstrom's office," Li said. "Which we have now done."

"You mean you actually suspected one of us?" Mignon asked.

"Certainly not. I suspected *both* of you. If I hadn't suspected two people who were at the scene on the night of the crime and had both access to the office and a motive to commit the theft, Harvard Law School would have confiscated my copy of *Wigmore on Evidence*."

"That is an outrageous imputation of someone with an unblemished academic record going back almost thirty years."

"Lawyers are paid to be pessimists," Li shrugged.

"And misanthropic cynics with no confidence in the integrity of their professional colleagues?"

"Yeah, that too. But that's a topic for another day. It's enough for the moment to know that Professor Pennyworth has nixed the possibility that either of you did it. If either of you had taken the document, you would have known that the page Professor

Pennyworth displayed this afternoon wasn't it. Hence, you wouldn't have reacted as you did."

"That strikes me as highly qualitative and non-rigorous," Mignon said.

"Oh come off it, dean," Melissa said. "Neither of you could have been faking it. You couldn't feign a leer in a strip club, and when it comes to guilelessness Ms. Bleifert makes Candide look like Machiavelli."

"In short," Li said. "don't worry, be happy. Your manifest ignorance acquits you."

"So we still don't know where the original of the real papal order is?"

"There is no real papal order," Melissa said. "At least Professor Angstrom never had one. There wasn't any papal document of any kind in the hymnal that he appraised, much less a written order that only a very foolhardy pontiff would have sent through Nazi-occupied territory where it would have meant a concentration camp—or worse—for anyone caught carrying it. His whole story about finding it was a fabrication."

"How can you be so sure of that?" Bleifert asked.

"If the pope had given a written order in 1943 to the abbot of a monastery in Czechoslovakia," Melissa said, "it wouldn't have been written in Italian. It would have been written in Latin. If I were twenty years older I would have realized that immediately instead of having to have my nose rubbed in it three or four times by Latin-spouting lawyers."

"Maybe," Mignon said. "But *someone* broke into Angstrom's office and stole *something*. Whoever did it must at least have *thought* it was valuable."

"No one broke into Angstrom's office," Melissa said. "He staged the forced entry and the ransacking before he left for the Brontë event, knowing that Tereska would discover it when she returned the Power Point equipment."

"Why would he have done that?" Bleifert asked.

"To avoid having to produce the original of the document. He had shown a photocopy to Taylor Gates and invented a story to make it seem real. Gates bit because he saw the marketing potential of a tie-in between a new thriller and headlines about a real-world controversy over a document like the one at the heart of his story. He paid Angstrom off by lending him the muscle and prestige of his own agent for a novel that Angstrom wanted to place. I'm guessing, however, that when Gates came to Milwaukee for the sex-or-swim trial he started pressing for a look at the original."

"Which Angstrom didn't have," Li said.

"The break-in gave him an excuse for not being able to produce it."

"But what about the gas thing at Villa Terrace?" Bleifert asked. "He and Gates were both attacked. Who did that?"

"That was a publicity stunt staged by Gates, in connivance with Angstrom. It fit in with a claim of death-threats that Gates was trying to use my husband to corroborate. The point was to generate attention that would ratchet up his sales."

"Then what it comes down to," Bleifert said, her voice a little harder now, "is that Professor Angstrom was selling fairy dust to someone he regarded as an intellectual lightweight but who had a lot more money than he did."

"That's a very charitable way to put it," Melissa said.

"So who killed him?"

"I don't know. But I know who *didn't* kill him—and that's enough for me."

PART FOUR
Shoot the Lawyer Twice

Q: It's 1933. You're in a locked room with Adolph Hitler, Joseph Stalin, and a lawyer. You have a revolver with two bullets in the cylinder. What do you do?

A: Shoot the lawyer twice.

—Popular Lawyer Joke

Chapter Twenty-eight

"Your halo is lovely, but you look completely spent."

"It was a very demanding meeting." Melissa handed her coat gratefully to Rep, then staggered into the living room and collapsed on the couch. "I had to affect a casual attitude while it was going on, but when it was finally over I hit an emotional wall."

"I put water on for tea when I heard your key in the door."

"Bless you."

"And I've made something special for dinner."

"What?"

"Reservations at Coquette."

"You are now officially the one with the halo."

"They're not until eight, so I'll draw you a bath with some of that stuff you have while you enjoy your tea. That way you can relax a bit before we need to leave."

A shrill whistle from the kitchen spared Rep further accusations of spousal sanctity. By the time he returned with a steaming mug of herbal tea, Melissa had taken her shoes off and propped her feet cross-ankled on the coffee table. Rep felt he could safely ask for details about the day.

"Mission accomplished." Before sipping the tea Melissa held the mug just in front of her mouth and let the aroma waft toward her nose. Then she gave him a quick summary.

"So first you got Bleifert to open up and now you've cleared her."

"Right. Now I'm sure she told me the truth."

"Therefore she had nothing to do with Angstrom's murder."

"Correct. Which means that my speculations about her mischief the night of the break-in couldn't shed any useful light on the killing."

"No need to share those conjectures with the police, then," Rep said.

"Right again."

"I'm comfortable with that, if you are."

"I am *so* comfortable with it." Melissa cradled the mug in her lap and lay her head back against the sofa cushion's crushed green leather. "I'm sorry that Angstrom was murdered and I feel for Valerie Clevenger, even though I wouldn't bet her son is innocent. But that's no excuse for turning into a—what's the legal term for busybody?"

"'Officious intermeddler.'"

"Right. I'm not going to turn into one of those. I wanted to make sure I didn't have a moral obligation to rat out Tereska Bleifert. I don't. End of story. Exit Melissa, stage right. The police now have center stage, and they're welcome to it."

"Exactly."

"You agree with me, then?"

"Yes."

Ten seconds of silence passed. Melissa lifted her head long enough to drink some tea, then laid it back again. Six more seconds passed. She opened her eyes without raising her head and shifted them toward Rep.

"What are you waiting for?" she asked. "In a 1940's movie, this would be the 'thanks, I needed that' scene, where a no-nonsense male tells the spunky heroine she's better than that and gives her a brisk little slap to punctuate his point."

"Spousal battery is out of fashion these days, especially with heroines spunky enough to hit back. More important, I really do think you're absolutely right. You've gone above and beyond the call of duty already. No need for you to make more blips on anyone's radar screen."

"Then why am I waiting for the other shoe to drop?"

"Um, yes. That. Well. The thing is, I've been looking for the right psychological moment to mention that Valerie Clevenger left a message asking that you call her."

"Hmm. I wonder what provoked that."

"Probably the approaching retrial date for her son's case."

"I don't see how I can help her with that. The only thing I can contribute is information, and the only information I have that she doesn't already know is something Tereska told me in absolute confidence."

"That should make for an interesting conversation."

"Interesting and short. Well, I can't face it right now. This heroine is taking a break from spunkiness for the rest of the night. After I finish this tea and take that bath you recommended, the most ambitious thing I'm going to do before we leave for Coquette is email my brother."

"I'll draw your bath. Lavender bath oil or vanilla?"

"Surprise me." Melissa's head sank back into the cushion with a delicious moan of anticipatory pleasure.

As the delicate lavender scent from the first elegant beads of oil splashing into running water rose toward Rep, Carolyn Hoeckstra's nose twitched at the stronger smell of a different type of oil. Rich and oddly sweet, the odor of Cosmoline seemed to surround her as she walked up and down rows of heavily laden tables in the Great Exhibition Hall at Wisconsin State Fair Park, about three freeway miles west of Milwaukee's baseball stadium.

She stopped at a table and picked up one of a dozen handguns displayed on it. The weapon was a small automatic, a Beretta thirty-two caliber. She looked at it, hefted it in the palm of her right hand, then seemed about to do something else with it when another gun caught her eye. She put down the Beretta and picked up a larger automatic with a back-slanting checkered grip.

"That's a Luger," a woman in a red-and-black plaid lumberjack shirt said from behind the table.

"I know. Replica?"

"It's a *genuine* replica," the heavyset lumberjill said after a moment's hesitation. "Manufactured by Charter Arms in the 'sixties to the original specs, with shop drawings traced from the original blueprints and tooling cast from the original molds."

Hoeckstra clicked the clip out and slid it back home, then pulled back the twin knurled knobs on top of the bolt. They snapped into a blunt triangle, leaving an extra two inches of deeply blued barrel exposed.

"So it would be nine millimeter?"

"Absolutely. A lot of knock-off replicas made in the 'sixties were twenty-two caliber, like for guys who just wanted something offbeat looking for plinking. But the ones Charter made are the real deal. They sent their machine shop manager and a master machinist to Essen—"

"Skip it," Hoeckstra said. "How much?"

"Seven-fifty."

"Sold." Handing the Luger to the lumberjill, Hoeckstra squatted to open an ancient, battered American Tourister attaché case with rounded corners that were thought to be chic in the early 'seventies. She took eight hundred-dollar bills and a business card from it and handed them to the woman behind the counter. "Write it up. And *don't* keep the change."

Transactions at gun shows in the United States aren't heavy on paperwork. The lumberjill dropped the Luger unceremoniously into a brown paper bag, together with a four-page pamphlet explaining its historical significance. She then pulled a pad of forms from next to a slotted cash-box behind the table and pinned the business card next to it with her left thumb so that she could look at it while she wrote. Next to NAME on the top form she carefully printed JANE SCHMIDT.

"You're spoiled rotten. You do realize that, don't you?"

"Yes, I do," Melissa said around seven twenty-five. she typed lcdrfxsetonusna@navy.mil into the email address box on her computer screen. "You are deeply appreciated. I feel like a million dollars, and I'll be ready to leave in five minutes."

She typed "Goodies" in the subject box, then tabbed to the message portion of the screen and typed:

Frank,

1 dzn brownies and 1 dzn Rice Krispie treats going out Monday. Should I add a box of Smores or would that be overdoing it? More later.

Love,

'Lissa

"Okay," she said as she hit SEND and stood up. "Let's go."

"Should we take the car or walk?"

"What is it outside?"

"Around thirty without much wind. And the sidewalks are pretty clear."

"Let's walk then," Melissa said. "It's less than half-a-mile."

"You're turning into a real Milwaukean."

Just after eight-twenty, as Rep was accepting *biftec au frites* from a waiter at Coquette, René Mignon thoughtfully riffled the pages of a paperback book. The cover featured a lurid picture of a woman wearing a badly ripped blouse and cowering before a snarling panther. The title, stamped on the cover in blood red letters, was *Pawn's Gambit*. "A New Thriller by Taylor Gates!" appeared above the title.

What to do? Mignon had an academic's aversion to destroying books. Leaving aside the occasional bit of French pornography, however, this was the first fiction he could remember reading in decades. Explaining why he happened to have a novel whose fourth chapter included a detailed description of how to come up with a lethal dose of curare might be a bit delicate.

A grating *whirr* filled Mignon's modest study as he turned on the paper shredder beside the desk. After a last glance at the cringing woman's *décolletage*, he ripped the cover off and fed it into the machine. Over eleven tedious minutes, each and every page would follow.

Glancing at her watch as she and Rep returned from Coquette, Melissa frowned. Nine-forty-eight. If it were ten o'clock she could tell herself that it was too late to call Clevenger.

Well, tough. Maybe tomorrow.

She flipped her computer on and went to look for something to glance at while it booted up. Sartre? No. She wasn't in the mood for someone who spent World War II snugly in Paris, scribbling plays that he tamely submitted to Nazi censors. She pulled down a volume of Malraux instead.

She made it through three bracing pages before her computer grudgingly beeped that it was ready to do computer stuff. She called up her emails, and the only non-spam entry was Lieutenant Commander Francis Xavier Seton's reply to her missive earlier in the evening:

SETON, LCDR FRANCIS

FROM: Lt. Com. Francis X. Seton
            [lcdrfxsetonusna@navy.mil]
SENT: Saturday, Jan 26, 2008 9:27 p.m.
TO: Melissa Seton Pennyworth [msp@uwm.edu]
SUBJECT: Goodies

Sis,

Toastable Oreo Pop Tarts are actually more popular right now than Smores, and a box or two would be welcome. Believe me, the treats you send are REALLY appreciated. Midshipmen call this period between Christmas and Easter "the Dark Ages." The weather is dreary, they're not going to see their families for months, some can't leave the Yard even on weekends, and the discipline is unrelenting. An Oreo Pop

Tart goes a long, LONG way.

I followed up with an 06 chem prof on that murder up there you were telling me about. He said that deriving a lethal dose of curare wouldn't be any particular trick if you had plenty of money and access to a decent college chem lab.

Love,

Frank

Melissa hit PRINT and looked over her shoulder while her printer coughed into action.

"Honey, are you in the kitchen?" she called

"No, but I can get there in about five seconds."

"Would you write Oreo Pop Tarts on the whiteboard please?"

"Sure."

Melissa closed her email window and started to log off her computer.

"Oreo what?" Rep yelled from the kitchen.

That's why we print emails. Melissa plucked the freshly-printed sheet from the printer.

"Oreo Pop Tarts."

She started to lay down the print-out, then suddenly stopped and gazed intently at the page. She was still studying it when Rep came in to report that he had completed his assignment. Noticing her close examination of the document he looked at it over her shoulder.

"Wouldn't a class of 2006 graduate be kind of young for a chemistry professor?"

"'Oh-six' refers to rank, not class year," she muttered distractedly. "It means a captain in the Navy or the Coast Guard and a colonel in the other three services. Frank is an oh-four."

"Oh."

Grabbing the phone, Melissa punched in Valerie Clevenger's number. Clevenger answered on the first ring.

"Sorry to return your call so late," Melissa said.

"Oh, that's all right. I hate to be a pest—"

"Not at all. Would two o'clock Saturday afternoon be convenient?"

"Of course."

"I'd come earlier, but I'm going to try to visit a doctor tomorrow morning."

"Two o'clock is no problem at all. I'll see you then. Goodnight."

After hanging up, Melissa looked down at André Malraux's prose, the work of someone who didn't just write about being *engagé* but had actually traded gunfire with Franco's soldiers and Hitler's stormtroopers.

"Thanks," she said. "I needed that."

Chapter Twenty-nine

The second Saturday in January, 2008

You suggest residential exclusivity to a Milwaukean by saying "North Shore." You suggest it to someone on the North Shore by saying "east of Lake Drive." The sliver of land between Lake Michigan and the highway named for it doesn't have streets but arcane "lanes" and "courts" and "places." When the favored souls who dwell there share their addresses with the *hoi polloi*, they tack on the four magic words—"Bridge Lane, east of Lake Drive," "North View Place, east of Lake Drive"—on the plausible assumption that without this additional clue simply naming the street wouldn't help much.

When Melissa turned right onto Shore Drive on Saturday afternoon and began looking for Valerie Clevenger's house, she was east of Lake Drive.

She checked her watch as she stopped at the crown of Clevenger's semi-circular driveway. She rummaged through six boxes of Oreo Pop Tarts in the plastic Sendiks grocery bag beside her on the front seat, in the process knocking two of them onto the floor. They fell onto a cheaply bound booklet with a yellow paper cover that was sternly marked in black block letters:

PAWN'S GAMBIT
By TAYLOR GATES

BOUND GALLEY
NOT FOR RESALE!

While retrieving the Pop Tarts she checked to be sure she hadn't lost the sales slip for the book, as she intended to deduct every penny of the six dollars she had shelled out for the thing. At length she returned to the Sendiks bag and extracted a palm-sized squeeze bottle of Chloraseptic Throat Spray with a white plastic cone attached to its top. Clevenger, dressed in khaki slacks and a yellow blouse cut like a man's dress shirt, already had the front door open and was striding out onto an ample porch to meet her.

"Sorry I'm late," Melissa said as she scurried to the porch. "I had a Nancy Northshore type in front of me in the checkout line, right down to the sweater with its sleeves tied around her neck. This week's *Cosmopolitan* promises a story about 'Seven Sex Tricks He'd Never *Dream* You Know!' and she seemed to be agonizing over whether to buy it."

"I hope she opted for erotic enrichment." Clevenger showed Melissa into a foyer floored in black and dove gray marble.

"She did, but in the time she took to decide she could just about have memorized the article."

After stashing her coat in a hall closet, Melissa followed Clevenger into the living room, where the color scheme on the marble changed to green and blue-veined white. She walked in expecting to see Eames chairs heavy on tautly stretched black leather and a coffee table with inch-thick glass and highly polished chrome. She didn't. Crayola-vivid red and blue leaped from the walls. Snow white and sable black area rugs shared the floor with green and yellow beanbag chairs. A set of hot pink Smartbelle walking weights sat on the white-brick perch beside the fireplace.

"It's something, isn't it?" Clevenger asked.

"Something? You're two bong hits away from *Yellow Submarine.*"

"I can do coffee, tea, or Johnny Walker Red. If that inhaler means you've picked up a sore throat I'll be happy to get some designer water from the kitchen, but if I were you I'd treat it with scotch instead."

"Tea. Please."

Melissa dosed herself with a quick spray of Chloroseptic while Clevenger fussed at a drink caddy. She handed Melissa fragrant herbal tea in what looked like a genuine Limoges cup, then took two fingers of amber liquid in a tumbler for herself. While Melissa felt her way tentatively onto a beanbag chair, Clevenger stretched deftly on her side, Madame Recamier-style, on a pile of Persian carpets six rugs thick next to the crackling fire place. She leaned her back against a seventh rug rolled tightly to form an oversized cushion.

"It took me seven years to get this room exactly the way I wanted it," she said. "I fired three decorators and finally just did it myself. The idea is that no one should ever imagine that a Nancy Northshore type lives here."

"You've certainly accomplished that."

Every word from Clevenger's mouth, every gesture, every detail of her welcome struck Melissa as polished and confident. At the same time, though, the gloss on her performance seemed as slickly professional as the polish on the finished marble around the fireplace, as if Melissa were a potential client whose business Clevenger was trying to get.

"I asked you to come over because I have a delicate and unpleasant question to ask," Clevenger said. "Could Carolyn Hoeckstra have gotten into Professor Angstrom's office the night of the break-in?"

"Not likely. The university is very security conscious. There's a guard desk at the only public entrance—and the guards know their business."

"Isn't there a faculty entrance that's unguarded?"

"Yes, but you have to have a pass card and know a numerical code that's changed daily. And even that entrance is under video surveillance."

"Suppose Hoeckstra had gotten Angstrom's card and code."

"How could she have managed that?"

"*Nisi bonum de mortui* and all that, but Jimmy says he was a leche."

"I've heard people call him a skirt-chaser," Melissa admitted.

"Hoeckstra can play the hottie when she wants to. Say she put a move on Angstrom, suggested that they hook up in his office, and asked for his card and code so that she could wait there while he showed off at Villa Terrace."

"Surely he would have told her that the horizontal surfaces would be more comfortable at his flat in Shorewood."

"Say he did. She responds that sex in unconventional venues turns her on. That's probably one of the seven tricks *Cosmo* was panting about."

"Okay." Melissa shrugged. "As long as we're just making things up, suppose she does say exactly that. And suppose he's so excited that his brain shuts off and he immediately starts thinking with his testicles."

"Which wouldn't exactly set a precedent with the male gender."

"Fair enough. Is Angstrom so besotted by lust in this hypothesis that he forgets he only has one key-card? If Hoeckstra takes his so that she can metaphorically warm up the sheets in his office while she's waiting for him, how is *he* going to get in?"

"He's a well-known professor, in and out of Curtin Hall every day. He can walk in the front door and stroll right past the security desk. He wouldn't even have to show i.d., much less swipe a pass-card."

"You've thought this through very carefully," Melissa said, nodding as she reviewed Clevenger's analysis. "It could have happened that way. Of course, the video surveillance at the faculty entrance would still have been a risk for Hoeckstra. When she got in using his card, the guard staffing the video monitors might still have noticed her."

"Sure. He would have noticed an apparently responsible adult who had a working card and knew the daily security code. There must be several hundred faculty and staff authorized to use that entrance. No guard could possibly knew them all by sight—certainly not well enough to sound an alarm based on a grainy image on a video screen. And even if she were challenged and a guard tracked her down, she'd shrug and say she was there to play slap-and-tickle with one of the eggheads."

"Absolutely right," Melissa said. "As far as it goes. In that scenario, Hoeckstra gets into his office without major risk. But the reason she wants to get there in your theory is to toss the place in search of evidence that might compromise the prosecution of your son, right?"

"Right. The most promising front in her vendetta against me."

"She hates you that much?"

"For polluting her father's bed? She hates me more than Captain Ahab hated the whale. Tim and I were mature adults with healthy sexual appetites, but she treated me like some seventeenth century cavalier who callously deflowered a maiden and besmirched the family escutcheon."

"Anyway," Melissa said, "she's in his office because she's after something. She has to know that sooner or later someone is going to notice the burglary. At that point the security tapes from that night will be reviewed."

"Yes, that is precisely the question."

"You just lost me."

Clevenger took a healthy sip of scotch. Bright-eyed, face glowing with a tinge of excitement, she levered herself forward to emphasize her next point.

"All video surveillance is not created equal. There are systems that use dummy cameras merely as a deterrent. There are systems that use real cameras running tape on a repeating sixty-minute loop, so that a guard with a monitor can see what's going on at any given moment but you can't retrieve tape of anything more than an hour in the past."

"Okay."

"And then, there are sophisticated and expensive digital video systems that store what the cameras record in large capacity computerized archives. I'm wondering whether UWM has one of those."

"I don't know. But even if it does I couldn't get it for you."

"I wouldn't ask you to. If we know it's there and we know what to ask for, we can get it with a subpoena."

"But what do you accomplish if you do? Suppose you prove that Carolyn Hoeckstra was in Curtin Hall that night. Confront her with that on the stand during your son's retrial and presumably she'll blow it off with the same lust-in-the-ivy line you said she would have used on an inquisitive guard. You can't use that tape to prove she ransacked his office."

"We don't have to. We're the defense. We're not required to prove anything. All we have to do is raise a reasonable doubt."

Melissa sat still for a moment. With an unladylike slurp that would have earned her a glare from her grandmother, she gulped tea without tasting it.

"And how does smearing Hoeckstra do that?" she asked then. "It makes her look bad, but it doesn't make Jimmy look good. Whatever the exculpatory information itself might be, you still don't have it."

"If you assume that Carolyn Hoeckstra went to great lengths to get evidence from Angstrom that was relevant to Jimmy's case, and if she doesn't produce that evidence herself, the jury will *presume* that the evidence would have hurt the government. In a perverse way, it's almost better for us *not* to have the actual evidence. That way the jury can just let its collective imagination run wild."

"I see," Melissa said.

"I know, it isn't pretty. But neither is thirty months in a federal penitentiary for a boy whose only crime is an exaggerated sense of entitlement."

"I get your point."

"Angstrom's murder has raised the stakes. We can't make a subpoena stick if it's based solely on supposition. But if we can say with a straight face that some electronic blips on a computer tape somewhere at UWM might reveal a murderer who killed a witness with potentially critical evidence, then I think we'll get a look at them. Will you find out for me what type of surveillance system UWM uses?"

"I'll have to think about it. To tell you the truth, I'm not very comfortable about collaborating in innuendo. Suppose I could come up with the evidence itself: would you settle for that?"

"What makes you think you could bring that off?"

"A hint of a theory that's been tickling the back of my brain since I found out that Angstrom was killed. He was apparently shopping two completely unrelated pieces of supposedly valuable information: a papal order dating from the Second World War, and the exculpatory facts you were looking for. The more I think about that, the more implausible it seems to me."

"I agree," Clevenger said. "He was a professor, not a spook with tentacles reaching into the CIA. It's hard enough to believe he came up with one of those, much less both of them. But where are you going with this?"

"Suppose they weren't unrelated. Suppose one was a cover for the other—camouflage."

"I'm supposing. That implies that if you find one you could find the other. But how do you get from supposition to proof?"

"That brings me to a delicate question of my own," Melissa said.

"I have thick skin and plenty of scotch. Shoot."

"Is it true that Gates is Jimmy's father?"

"Yes. If you'll forgive me, I'll skip any maidenly blush over that confession. I'm not ashamed of it."

"I wouldn't suggest that you should be."

"It wasn't a casual fling, if that makes any difference. He was working in Houston when his break-out book hit it big. I liked his early stories that I pulled off the regional paperback racks. I thought his writing had some guts to it. I wanted a kid, my biological clock was ticking, I didn't have the time or the taste to dig up a husband, and I thought having some creative genes in my offspring would be a kick. I figured that Robert Ludlum was busy so I tracked Gates down and asked him how he'd like to have a groupie for a month or so."

"Well, that's plain enough."

"I know. I make those calculating dowagers in Jane Austen's novels seem like sentimentalists. But that's neither here nor there. How much money do you need from Gates to prove your theory?"

"I don't need any money. I need to ask him two questions— and I need him to tell me the truth."

Chapter Thirty

The third Friday in January, 2008

"Please don't tell me you're trying to get a thriller published too," were Taylor Gates' first words when he called Melissa almost a week later.

"The only thing I'm trying to get published at the moment is a piece on Trollope's unacknowledged influence on the contemporary American action/adventure story. Using violence to blend politics into literature and vice-versa. I don't think Amy Lee would be much help with it."

"Don't underestimate her."

"So you heard about my theory concerning the late Professor Angstrom's venture into popular fiction," Melissa said.

"I have instructions to answer two questions. Is that the first one?"

"No. This is the first one: In the bound galleys of *Pawn's Gambit* that your publisher circulated as advance copies to reviewers, you had a murder committed by substituting a poison for a prescription drug the victim was taking. Not terribly original, but more elegant than just smearing curare on a hash pipe, which is the way the murder is committed in the version of the book actually published. Why the change?"

"That's a rather embarrassing question."

"I'm told your ego is healthy enough to handle it."

"Okay. We sent the galleys around to prominent mystery and thriller authors, looking for blurbs. One of our targets was a doctor, although he's now pursuing a different career. Short, round-faced, bright-eyed, and puckish, with a very dry wit. He declined to give me a blurb, but he told me the drug-substitution trick wouldn't work."

"Why not?"

"Prescription drug manufacturers are very particular about the shape, color, size, and texture of their products. They deliberately make them as distinctive as they can, precisely because they want to cut down on the risk of taking the wrong drug by mistake."

"So you couldn't just, say, buy a pack of Contac off the shelf, replace the cold medicine in the capsules with something toxic, and then substitute one of the doctored capsules for the prescription drugs the victim was taking."

"Right," Gates said. "The victim would know something was wrong. You'd have to somehow get your hands on some of the actual drugs, put the poison in them, and then get them back without the victim knowing it. I would have had to write an entire new chapter to make that work. It was simpler to just shoehorn some happy-hay into the story."

"Second question: What's the narrative plausibility of someone obsessed with Catholicism going to a lot of trouble to kill a victim inside a basilica?"

"Zero. That's the kind of bullshit that happens in cheap thrillers by lazy writers instead of in the real world. Just out of curiosity, where did that question come from?"

"I think Timothy Goettinger was murdered. I think the same person who killed Professor Angstrom killed him."

"Okay. Two questions asked, two answered. Does Valerie get the inside details about UWM's security camera system?"

"Yes. You held up your end of the bargain, so I won't renege on mine. I don't expect to go to confession anytime soon, but you can't be too careful."

◇◇◇

Kuchinski was busily getting ready to defend Q Kazmaryck when Melissa stopped by the Germania Building later that afternoon to tell him and Rep about her conversation with Taylor Gates. Kuchinski whistled when she was through.

"Making that crack to him was about as subtle as cold-cocking him with a kielbasa."

"Subtlety isn't my strong point."

"So how do you put it together?"

Melissa explained her theory to the two lawyers.

"Have you shared this with Chicago's finest?" Kuchinski asked.

"As much as I could, without implicating Tereska or revealing information I'd promised to keep confidential."

"I take it they are *not* sending their most tactful senior detective up here to ask Milwaukee cops to arrest someone for them."

"Not exactly. They thanked me for my concern and assured me they would factor this information into their inquiries."

"'Don't worry your pretty little head about it,' in other words."

"I can't really blame them. Amateur speculation isn't evidence, and aside from Frank's email I had precious little more than that to offer them."

"And if the killer nails someone else while they're processing all this data," Rep said, "well, that would be outside their jurisdiction anyway."

Kuchinski stretched luxuriantly, spreading his arms into a gargantuan V and swiveling his chair so that he could extend his legs completely in front of him. The process took several seconds. Then he pulled back to a more lawyerly pose, folded his hands on top of his desk blotter, and looked from Rep to Melissa and back again.

"So what it comes down to is that we're pretty sure what happened, but we're missing a few exhibits from our evidence folder."

"Quite a few," Rep said.

"And we don't have any way of getting the proof we need to back us up."

"Not that I can see," Melissa said.

"Well, then," Kuchinski said, picking up his phone and punching a speed-dial button, "I guess we'd better make some up."

Expecting Kuchinski to reach a secretary or voice-mail, Rep was surprised at the next words out of the older lawyer's mouth.

"Terry? Walt Kuchinski. Can I put you on speaker? I've got co-counsel in the office with me."

The answer must have been yes, because Kuchinski punched another button and Finnegan's voice almost immediately came over the speaker.

"Your boy finally ready to plead?"

"Nope."

"Then what's on your mind?"

"The local rule calls it meet-and-confer. We're supposed to chat about certain motions before I file them. And to tell you the truth, I'd want you to see this one before I filed it anyway."

"What's it about?"

"It's about you. Specifically, about bouncing your butt off this case so that you can go after drug-dealers and rum-runners like the founding fathers intended and let someone else handle Jimmy Clevenger's little problem with keeping his fly zipped."

"Any grounds?" Finnegan asked in jovial and slightly bored voice. "Or are you just asking for disqualification on general principles?"

"Well for starters, we're fixing to make you a witness—and last time I checked there was a rule about that."

"There's a rule about filing frivolous motions, too."

"Trust me on this one, son. We've gotta talk. Face to face. You really do want to see me."

"Okay. How about tomorrow morning, first thing?"

"See ya then."

Kuchinski hung up. He bowed his head for just a moment. Then he looked up.

"We're looking at long night."

"Anything I can do to help, besides ordering the pizza?" Rep asked.

"You know how to draft an offer of proof?"

"Yep."

"Okay. You do that and I'll do the motion."

Kuchinski picked up his Dictaphone as Rep and Melissa left.

"All right," Melissa said, "we'd better get to work."

"What do you mean 'we?'"

"Hey, I may not know any law but I know how to type. I'm the troublemaker here."

"True on both counts," Rep conceded as they stepped into his office, "but aren't you supposed to be finding out what type of surveillance system UWM uses so you can keep your promise to Valerie Clevenger?"

"I pinned that information down about an hour ago. Li was right: in dealing with bureaucracies, few commodities are more precious than the gratitude of lawyers."

"What's the answer?"

"The one she was hoping for: the recordings on UWM's security cameras are digitally made and computer-retrievable."

"When are you going to tell her?"

"As soon as you hand me your phone. I'll leave word on her answering machine at home, and I bet she calls back to react and follow up within twenty-four hours."

Chapter Thirty-one

The first Wednesday in February, 2008

Fortunately, Melissa didn't give long odds. Instead of a phone call the next day she got a personal visit almost two weeks later, first thing on a cloudy Wednesday morning.

"I hope I'm not intruding," Clevenger said as she squeezed into Melissa's office after an apologetic knock. "First, I wanted to thank you for the data about the surveillance system. More important, I got a telephone message last night that I felt I should share with you. We've served a subpoena for the tapes, and I think this call is clearly a reaction to it."

"'Politics as Metaphor and Metaphor as Politics in Trollope' can wait for a few minutes." Melissa looked up from a sheaf of typescript. "Please sit down."

"Thank you."

Unholstering her cell phone, Clevenger punched numbers and prompts and laid the instrument on Melissa's desk. After a couple of seconds of white- noise blur, a crackly voice that sounded like it had bounced off four satellites started speaking.

"Hoeckstra. I want to talk, and I think you'll be interested in what I have to say. Face to face. Has to be someplace no one would ever expect to see either of us, so unless you have a better idea let's make it St. Josephat's Basilica. Where my dad bought it, in case you've forgotten. Do *not* bring your horny little brat.

I don't know if they have a noon mass on weekdays, but if they do it should be cleared out by one. I'll be there at five after tomorrow. Pew nearest the confessional. Call back if you're not going to show. And if you do call back, note that the area code is nine-two-oh, not four-one-four."

"Hmm," Melissa said.

"Right."

"What do you think she has in mind?"

"I think she wants to make a deal on my son's case. Fear trumps hatred."

"Fear of what?"

"Being implicated in Professor Angstrom's murder."

"You believe Hoeckstra thinks you have a line on evidence tying her to Angstrom's killing?"

"Right. I think she's afraid that if I get the tape showing her entering Curtin Hall on the night of the break-in, I'll be able to connect it to the damaging information Angstrom had and land her hip-deep in a homicide investigation."

"So if you're right, at five after one tomorrow afternoon Hoeckstra will offer to let Jimmy off the hook if you'll stop going after this hypothetical incriminating evidence—is that the idea?"

"Yes. She can tell Finnegan that she doesn't want to face the psychological trauma of another trial. He'd pretty much have to let Jimmy off with a wrist-slap that wouldn't brand him as a sex offender or send him to prison. I'd no longer have any reason to try to prove that she killed Angstrom to suppress evidence that would help Jimmy, so I'd stop trying."

"The only complication being that, tape or no tape, you don't actually have the lead on the Angstrom information that she thinks you do."

"Which isn't a complication as long as she thinks I do have it."

"So you'd make the deal?" Melissa asked.

"Of course. I'd make the deal even if I did have the evidence. Jimmy is more important to me than justice for a dead professor."

"You haven't considered going to the police?"

"The police are trying to put my son in a single-gender dance hall for two to three years."

"You don't sound like you're suggesting a debate, so I won't argue with you," Melissa said. "Just for the record, I think you're showing poor judgment."

"Noted."

"If your mind is made up, though, why are you telling me?"

"Because my whole theory could be dead wrong," Clevenger said crisply. "Maybe she doesn't want to make a deal at all. Maybe she has a completely different agenda. Listen to the message again. Focus on the last part."

Clevenger played the voice-mail back. Melissa frowned in concentration as the closing sentence crackled over the tiny speaker.

"'Note that the area code....'" Melissa repeated. "Is that what you mean?"

"Yes. I'm betting the phone she used to call with this message is one of those things with prepaid minutes that you can pick up at Wal-Mart. She had to drive at least to Sheboygan County to get one with a nine-two-oh area code. If she paid cash for it there'd be no way to trace the number to her."

"What would that accomplish?"

"If she couldn't be tied to the phone or the message she could deny leaving the message for me at all, and claim that the meeting was my idea instead of hers. After all, you've heard the message twice. Could you swear under oath that it's Hoeckstra's voice?"

"No, I guess I couldn't," Melissa said. "But what difference does it make which one of you proposed the meeting?"

"She'd want it to look like I called for the meeting if she's setting me up for a witness-tampering charge—a claim that I tried to save Jimmy by threatening her or bribing her. Not that I have delusions of grandeur, but that's uncomfortably close to the way Clarence Darrow got framed for jury-tampering during a labor-terrorism trial in the 'twenties."

"Okay, I guess," Melissa said. "But how do you defuse that trap by telling me about it in advance?"

"I don't. Doing that accomplishes nothing. If you feel like going to St. Josephat's for the tail end of noon mass, on the other hand, I'd be happy to have your company—and that would accomplish a great deal."

Chapter Thirty-two

In Federalist Paper Number 1 Alexander Hamilton wrote, "I affect not reserves which I do not feel. I will not amuse you with an appearance of deliberation, when I have decided."

Well, Alexander Hamilton wasn't a trial lawyer. At nine-twenty-two on that same February morning, sitting beside Q Kazmaryck at the defense table in Courtroom Six-thirteen of the Milwaukee County Courthouse, Walt Kuchinski was affecting reserves that he didn't feel: scratching his head, poring over the computer print-out of the jury list with a worried frown, and otherwise suggesting an appearance of deliberation even though he had in fact decided, ten minutes ago, that the stiff in the suit had to go.

At last he squared the jury list in front of him. He bent his head toward Kazmaryck for a moment's final consultation. He nodded again, as did Kazmaryck. Then, as if with great reluctance, he drew a line through the stiff's name and next to it scribbled Δ#3, formally identifying the stiff as the defendant's third peremptory strike from the pool of potential jurors.

As Boone Fletcher in the spectator section watched the clerk take the jury list from Kuchinski and show it to the fresh-faced assistant district attorney, his first thought was that the ADA was a damn child. A baby. Fletcher had condoms that were older than that kid. His second thought was that he hadn't made a lot of progress recently on the Angstrom/sex-or-swim *et cetera* story, and he wasn't likely to make much more if Q got his silly butt hauled off to the House of Corrections for six months when this trial was over, which at the moment looked rather likely.

The clerk called out the names of the twelve jurors who'd survived the cut. The judge dismissed the rest of the panel and told the ADA to begin his opening statement. Fletcher guessed that he ought to pay attention, so he sighed and tried to focus on the courtroom.

At nine thirty-six a.m., Hoeckstra worked the last of six nine millimeter cartridges into the Luger's clip. She'd found the unfamiliar task surprisingly difficult the first couple of times she'd tried it, but after burning two boxes of bullets at an indoor shooting range she felt well practiced now, and slid the ammunition deftly into place. Then she inserted the clip into the Luger's stock and pushed it home until a solid CLICK announced that it was in position, ready to feed the chamber.

Naturally, she put the safety on. That's the kind of thing engineers do.

At ten o'clock sharp, Rep frowned as he retrieved Melissa's voice-mail. He frowned first of all because the Contac he'd taken that morning hadn't done a thing for his stuffy nose, and secondly because every word in the voice-mail except "dearest" bothered him.

Nevertheless, five minutes later he was dialing Kuchinski's cell-phone number. Kuchinski was in court and would have his cell-phone turned off, but Rep figured he would check messages during the morning recess.

"This is Rep. I suddenly need to get to Saint Josephat's over the noon hour. I checked Mapquest but it looks like they're taking me there by the same route the Third Crusade used to get to the Holy Land. So if you can get me a south side travel tip sometime in the next hour, I'd appreciate it."

◇◇◇

At ten-fifteen a.m., patrolman Thad Obendoerfer of the Milwaukee Police Department took the stand in Courtroom Six-thirteen. He testified that around five-thirty in the morning on a date late last December, in the vicinity of four-eleven South Chicago Street, he had seen a man crouched in front of the main door of the erotic bookstore at that address. The man turned out to be the defendant, Quintus Ultimusque Kazmaryck, who had traces of iron filings on his fingertips. Quantities of iron filings had also been introduced into the lock of the porn shop's door, and beyond suggesting that this was a remarkable coincidence, the defendant had had no explanation for any of these facts. Further investigation revealed that the owners of four other shops in the neighborhood discovered that iron filings had disabled their locks.

Kuchinski had no questions.

The ADA then called the manager of the smut shop, who looked like the manager of a smut shop. He testified that when he tried to open the front door of his establishment on the morning in question he had found the lock jammed by iron filings. When he'd locked up the night before, the lock was working fine.

Kuchinski had no questions. The prosecution rested. Kuchinski said that he'd like to make a motion.

"I thought you might," the judge sighed.

After the clerk ushered the jury out, Kuchinski moved to dismiss the charges against Kazmaryck with prejudice because the prosecution had failed to prove venue. He noted that there are lots of South Chicago Streets *outside* Milwaukee County. Hence, proving that Kazmaryck had done something suspicious on that street didn't necessarily mean he'd done anything at all in the City and County of Milwaukee.

The young ADA opined sarcastically that Milwaukee police officers weren't in the habit of conducting early morning street patrols in other cities. Kuchinski sprang to his feet, a package of Xeroxed cases in his left hand.

"Skip it," the judge said. "Motion granted. You don't prove venue in a criminal case by asking the jury to assume that the police were doing their job properly. You prove it by asking the cop, 'Is that the four-eleven South Chicago Street in the City and County of Milwaukee?' No guesswork. Case dismissed."

If Q was expecting congratulations for successfully navigating the shoals and reefs of the American criminal justice system, he was disappointed. After disgustedly gathering up his papers, Kuchinski stalked toward the courtroom exit and glared over his shoulder at Kazmaryck.

"What would your father do if he were alive today and knew you pulled a stunt like that?" he asked once they were in the corridor.

"He would kick my ass," Kazmaryck conceded gamely.

"And a waste of damn good shoe leather that would be."

"I hope you're not charging me for this rebuke," Kazmaryck said.

"I'm not only charging you, I view this as a value-billing situation."

Kuchinski dropped his trial bag on the floor and whipped out his cell-phone. Kazmaryck looked hopefully in the direction of Fletcher, who was approaching.

"Seriously, Q, how could you do anything so goddamn stupid? If they hadn't put some kid fresh out of Marquette on this thing you'd be eating baloney sandwiches for lunch from now until Labor Day."

"Give me a break, scribbler. Times are hard. Campaign finance money doesn't go as far as it used to. The election boards have accountants now. I'm a locksmith. I was just trying to generate a little demand to keep my skills from getting rusty. Don't think of it as burglary; think of it as business development."

Kazmaryck would have continued in this vein for several more paragraphs, but Fletcher suddenly shushed him. He braced himself against the marble wall and, oblivious to the pimp six feet to his left and the wife-beater a yard to his right, stared across the corridor in a kind of trance while his mind raced. Kazmaryck was certain that no sensory data could have penetrated the metaphysical fog surrounding Fletcher at that moment, but he was wrong. Fletcher did hear Kuchinski talking into his cell-phone.

"St. Josephat's, huh? Well, here's what you do. Don't take the freeway. Just get onto Sixth Street and turn south. There's a brand new bridge over the Menomonee River Valley, and Mapquest probably hasn't gotten the memo yet. That'll take you practically to the front door. You'll wanna give yourself twenty minutes to be safe, so leave about twelve-thirty."

"Are you all right, scribbler?" Kazmaryck asked anxiously. "You're not flashing back to some of the drugs you did when you were a scribbling major at Madison, are you?"

Fletcher ignored him. He took out his own cell-phone, punched in a number without looking at it and raised it to his face.

"This is Fletcher....*Boone* Fletcher, the famous reporter. I'm one of your goddamn *employees*. I'll need a photographer to meet me at St. Josephat's."

Chapter Thirty-three

"Thirty-five minutes," Melissa whispered to Clevenger as the priest and servers left the altar at St. Josephat's. "Not quite as snappy as the masses Henry the Fourth's chaplain managed, but not bad."

"Was it Henry the Fourth who said Paris is worth a mass?"

"Yes. He became Catholic so that he could be king of France. His chaplain got daily mass done in twenty minutes flat. Short sermons."

"I guess you have to know what you want." Clevenger suddenly swiveled in the pew and pointed toward the back of the church. "Is that Finnegan over there?"

Startled, Melissa turned to look in the same direction. She felt a thud at her feet and heard the rattle of metal and plastic against flagstone.

"What an oaf," Clevenger said with a schoolmarmish cluck. "I knocked your purse off the pew." She bent over to recover it.

"I don't see anyone who looks like Finnegan," Melissa said as she scrutinized the knots of exiting congregants. "Was he going out?"

"No, I thought I saw him coming in. No sign of him now. I think I'm just jumpy. We don't usually do clandestine meetings in white collar criminal defense. Sorry about your purse."

"No problem."

"It was a good idea to get us here half-an-hour early. The wait is giving me a chance to calm down."

"It comes from studying hard-boiled private eye novels," Melissa said. "The savvy, street-smart detective invariably gets a call about meeting a key witness at some out-of-the way place at a certain time. He always gets there right when he's told to so that he can be predictably ambushed by bad guys. You'd think that just once one of these gumshoes would show up thirty minutes early to scope things out."

They were speaking in muted voices, just above a whisper. Melissa glanced around the basilica, quiet now except for footfalls echoing from the floor. She counted at least two-dozen people still in the nave, from widows lighting candles to spring their husbands from Purgatory to a cohort of bundled street people huddling here and there, presumably more interested in the basilica's heating system than its spiritual grandeur.

No trivial number, but they seemed lost in the church's vast space, insignificant specks in the gothic light that bravely challenged the dim interior. An icy chill painted Melissa's gut. The phone-message had talked about a public place for this meeting, but the basilica suddenly didn't seem to qualify.

Rep, at that moment, would have welcomed a touch of sheltering dimness. He was trying to stay inconspicuous, but as his watch ticked toward one and the crowd on St. Josephat's steps rapidly thinned he didn't think he was managing it. Although he was doing his best to look as if he were admiring the architecture or absorbing the ambience or something vaguely spiritual like that, he sensed that his pose was transparent. He imagined some cherubic altar boy striding up in cassock and surplice to expose his imposture by challenging him sternly to make the sign of the cross.

HEL-LO.

Rep's eyes snapped all the way open. No sign of Gates or Mignon or Finnegan, but Hoeckstra's satin black Lincoln Navigator pulled into the church's parking lot, crunching effortlessly over the snow and ice accumulated there. He recognized the license plate number and, as the vehicle swung right into a parking space ten yards from the door, he spotted Hoeckstra at the wheel. Her blond hair shook impatiently above a parka with a blaze-orange tint that Rep associated with deer hunting and the deck crews of aircraft carriers.

Focused on Hoeckstra, Rep didn't notice Boone Fletcher and a rotund black guy in a Navy pea coat and watch cap get out of a well worn Civic at the far end of the lot. The black guy had a camera with a very long lens.

Rep backed up three steps to just inside the doorway, where he hoped the relative darkness would hide him while he kept Hoeckstra in sight. She climbed down from the Navigator to the packed snow on the parking lot. She started to slam the door behind her, then seemed to think better of it and turned back toward the SUV's interior. Rep's pulse quickened as he watched what happened next. Hoeckstra set her purse on the front seat, opened it, and casually transferred a pistol from the purse to her parka's right pocket.

Firearms definitely weren't in today's script. His mind raced. Had Melissa miscalculated? Was this Freud run amok? Love-hate thing with dad, killed him so the mom-substitute couldn't have him, then aced Angstrom because he tumbled to it? Melissa didn't go much for psychobabble, but sometimes the shrinks were onto something.

Didn't matter. The gun made the situation bad, and the closer that gun came to Melissa the worse it would get. *So much for inconspicuous.* Rep strode down the front steps, breaking into a trot so that he could intercept Hoeckstra before she got out from between the Navigator and a venerable Pontiac parked beside it. He blocked her path with two steps to spare.

"Move it or lose it, shorty," she said with dismissive impatience after a moment's startled glance.

"Five-nine is average height for European males," Rep protested mildly. "More important, we need to talk."

"Talk to this."

"This" was a left shoulder block that she threw into his chest as she moved to step past him. Rep staggered backward, slipped, and nearly fell. Barely keeping his feet, he managed to stay in her path. They were now just beyond the Navigator's bumper—and thus just within Fletcher's field of vision.

"What's your problem?" Hoeckstra demanded.

"The gun in your pocket."

She gaped at him. Neither of them noticed the rapid-fire clicks from the motor drive on the photographer's camera forty feet away.

"A stalker," she said with a who'd-believe-it shrug. "I suppose I should be flattered."

"Look," Rep said patiently, "why don't you just lock the gun in your SUV, where it will at least be technically legal for a few minutes, and I'll get out of your way and pretend I never saw it?"

"I stopped worrying about 'legal' when I buried my father. Show me a badge or back off."

"I can't do either one."

She stepped decisively to slice past Rep on his left. He swung his arm out to block her and caught a sharp elbow in the solar plexus for his trouble. This jolted him but instead of the full-fledged retreat Hoeckstra was expecting he snapped his arms at her and pushed back. Hoeckstra followed up with a forearm shiver to his collar bone. Rep stumbled backward and skidded on an icy patch. His fanny, back, and head hit the frosty pavement in that order. His glasses and cap went flying off behind him.

"You gettin' everything, Cyclops?" Fletcher asked the photographer.

"Hey, I get *paid* to do this."

"Good. A stuffed shirt pratfall might make page one."

Rep scrambled to his knees and reached out to grab Hoeckstra's leg as she scurried to get past him. He managed to get a throbbing right shoulder into her thighs and, more important, to slap at her handbag with his left hand and knock it off her arm, halfway back to the Navigator's door. As she backpedaled amid a stream of fluent obscenities to get it, Rep used the respite to half crawl and half crab-walk into the confined space between the vehicles. This delayed Hoeckstra's progress by about three seconds and kept Fletcher's jovial mood from being spoiled; for the Navigator now blocked his view of the proceedings. He couldn't see Hoeckstra pull the gun out of her pocket and swing it down in a rapid and abbreviated arc.

The side of the pistol smashed into Rep's left temple. His head jerked up and his mouth snapped open. He toppled sideways against the Navigator and then face-down onto the parking lot's surface. He probably would have yelled if he'd still been conscious, but he wasn't.

Fletcher and Cyclops saw Hoeckstra stalk back into view and march toward the church. Cyclops dutifully recorded the strut at three frames per second and enjoyed every moment of it. After Hoeckstra had gotten all the way to the church door without any reappearance by Rep, however, he lowered the camera and glanced uneasily at Fletcher, who was now following Hoeckstra.

"Maybe we should check on the guy first?" Cyclops inflected his voice to make it a question.

"Do I look like Richard Harding Davis to you?"

"If he was an aging hippie with a Christ-complex you could be his twin brother."

"He was a superstar reporter who got personally involved in his stories. I don't."

Cyclops looked back toward Navigator, where he still didn't see any signs of life.

"You know what, homey? Up yours."

Holding his camera around the barrel of the lens so that it wouldn't bang against his chest, he began loping gingerly toward the Navigator.

"All right, have it your way," Fletcher sighed as he turned to follow the photographer. "But if news happens in that basilica while you're busy posing for holy cards, I'm gonna discombobulate your f-stops."

Blissfully unaware that her husband's oozing blood was staining the snow outside, Melissa stiffened as she heard Hoeckstra's rapid footsteps striding up the aisle. Hoeckstra walked one pew past Melissa and Clevenger, then wheeled around to confront them. Cheeks flushed with chill and adrenaline, she took a couple of deep breaths before leaning forward to brace her hands against the back of the pew in front of the two women. She addressed them in a throaty stage whisper.

"All right, it's your party. Tell me why I'm here."

"I assume you're here to talk about getting this mess behind us," Clevenger said coolly as she cast a *did-I-call-this-or-what?* glance at Melissa. "We won round one. You won round two. How about we just call it a draw now, before round three gets nasty?"

"What's that supposed to mean?"

"Why is Professor Angstrom dead?"

"I don't know."

"Good answer. I don't either. Let's call it quits and keep it that way."

"Or else you accuse me of killing Angstrom when the case is tried again—is that what you're saying?"

"Certainly not," Clevenger cooed. "Saying that would make this conversation uncomfortably close to a felony. I'm saying that if whoever killed Angstrom was trying to suppress evidence in the sex-or-swim case, they failed. I have it."

"What is it?"

"You'll hear it when the jury does—if you really don't know."

"*If?*"

"Save it." Clevenger's voice suggested boredom with amateur theatrics. "Look, we've had tragedy enough. You've made your point. You've put Jimmy through more than enough hell to punish him for being a clod. Let's do a walk-away and get on with our respective lives."

"That clod came onto my ship in open water after midnight and tried to rape me," Hoeckstra said through fiercely clenched teeth, her tone all the more ferocious because she kept her voice low. "He threatened to throw me into the drink. If you think—"

"Wasn't that what you'd planned on him doing?" Melissa asked.

"*WHAT?*" Hoeckstra's head snapped toward Melissa's face.

"You made sure he knew about the party and you let him come on board. You waited for him to come on too strong, and when he did you dove into the lake like a blushing maiden afraid of a fate worse than death. You weren't afraid and we both know it. I'm not saying he's blameless. I'm just saying you wanted what happened to happen."

"I set him up? You're blaming the victim? That's the kind of crap I'd expect from a misogynist like Angstrom, not someone who owes her career to feminism."

"Save the guilt trip for some feminist who wrote her dissertation on angst induced by patriarchy. I got my degrees the old-fashioned way, so I don't have to take my opinions pre-packaged from the thought police. Facts are facts. You wanted to hurt Valerie, so you went after her son. The Jimmy thing was about you squaring things with dad, and Betty Friedan is no more help to you than she would have been to Hamlet."

In a furious hiss Hoeckstra told Melissa to perform an anatomically impossible sex act.

"Don't need to," Melissa shrugged. "I'm a happily married woman."

Slightly dampening the pleasure Melissa took in this riposte was the fear that it was wasted on Hoeckstra, who was whipping out of sight in ostentatious rage. Melissa took advantage of the diversion to glance to her right at the pew directly across the transept. Tereska Bleifert knelt there, eyes apparently focused on the altar—but not too focused to keep her from giving Melissa a barely perceptible nod.

"A frank and candid exchange of views," Clevenger said. "Thanks for jumping in and backing me up. It just might have done the trick. Hoeckstra isn't stupid. Once she has calmed down, she'll connect the dots and maybe we'll get something done."

"I wouldn't count on it."

"I've seen it happen before. Claiming to have the Angstrom stuff was pure bluff. But she wouldn't have asked for the meeting if she didn't think it might be true."

"She didn't ask for the meeting," Melissa said.

"What?"

"Wait a minute," Melissa said then.

She pulled herself abruptly to her feet. Three quick steps brought her to the confessional. Pausing for dramatic effect, she flung open the door of the nearer penitent's booth. Then she gasped and stepped back so quickly that she almost stumbled. This reflected not superior acting skills, for Melissa's were average at best, but genuine shock. Instead of the empty interior she had expected, she saw Assistant Dean René Cyntrip Mignon's trembling features. He recovered first.

"A punchline to an old joke in this situation would go, 'No, professor, *I* am surprised; *you* are astonished.'"

"Let's just skip that one," Melissa suggested.

"Good idea."

"What are you doing here? And please don't say you were waiting to go to confession."

"I was looking for the papal order."

"In a confessional?"

"In your conversation with Ms. Clevenger." A desperately avid glint lit Mignon's eyes. "I'm certain you do know where it is. I read all of Taylor Gates' novels looking for clues and hints, but I couldn't find any. A few years ago, Angstrom circulated an email asking for directions to this place, even though he had no earthly reason for visiting any church, much less a basilica. When I learned that you were meeting secretly with someone here, I thought I might overhear something that would tell me where to find it."

THERE IS NO BLOODY PAPAL ORDER! Melissa wanted to scream. THERE NEVER WAS! IT WAS A CON, YOU MORON!

But a glance at his face told her that saying this would be as futile as telling Sir Percival there was no holy grail, or assuring St. Helen that the True Cross had certainly gone to kindling centuries before she "found" it. She and Angstrom between them had done too good a job of selling their snake oil. Mignon was beyond logic, beyond common sense, irretrievably drunk on heady draughts of apodictic certainty. She chose instead to say something less dramatic but more practical under the circumstances.

"I think you should go. I understand the university's general counsel is about to circulate a memorandum with non-gender-neutral language."

"Oh dear. Yes, I suppose I should."

With surprising dignity, all things considered, Mignon stepped out of the confessional, nodded politely to Clevenger, and began to walk toward the rear of the church. After a few steps his pace quickened, as if he felt spurred on by the urgency of his new mission.

Melissa took another quick glance inside. Then, after a deep breath, she stepped into the booth, letting the door swing shut behind her. She didn't dwell on the grade school memories that suddenly flooded her head. Instead she got to work on the task that Mignon's unexpected presence had delayed. When Clevenger opened the door two minutes later she saw Melissa feeling tentatively around the corners, nooks, crannies, and niches of the cramped interior. Clevenger squeezed in next to Melissa. The door had just enough room to close behind them.

"Are you all right?" Clevenger whispered.

"Aside from raging paranoia and feeling a bit silly, I guess I am."

"What are you doing?

"Checking for electronics—and not finding any. Let's go back."

Clevenger opened the door, turned awkwardly, and stepped out of the confessional. Melissa emerged in her turn and followed Clevenger back toward the pew.

"Why were you checking for bugs?"

"Because, as I said just before I stumbled over Dean Mignon, Hoeckstra didn't set up this meeting."

"You're going to have to explain."

"Whoever left you that message gave the area code as 'nine-two-oh.' Hoeckstra is an anal retentive, by-the-numbers engineer. She makes Nurse Ratchet in *One Flew Over the Cuckoo's*

Nest look like Maria Montessori. For her, 'oh' is a letter, not a number. She'd never say 'oh' if she meant 'zero.'"

"And the message specified the pew nearest the confessional."

"Right."

"So there might be another bad guy—or gal—running around in this mess who manipulated both Hoeckstra and me into this meeting and maybe wanted to record what we said for posterity."

"Or for a grand jury," Melissa said.

"Ouch. I'm beginning to regret that 'verging on felony' crack."

A piercing contralto sliced through the ecclesial quiet before they could take the conversation further.

"Professor Pennyworth!" Mignon shouted from just inside the church doorway. "Outside, right away! It's your husband!"

"Jesus!" Melissa hissed. She realized with a spark of surprise as she raced toward the door that the word wasn't blasphemy but prayer.

Chapter Thirty-four

Mignon didn't wait for them, but Melissa didn't need his help to know where to go once she reached the front steps. An ambulance had backed into place to form a right angle with the Navigator's right rear bumper, and a knot of people had gathered around the scene. Melissa saw Rep lying on a gurney. A siren in the distance hinted that a policeman might soon be joining them.

"REPPPP!" Melissa screamed as she hurtled across the parking lot. Rep lifted his head from the gurney and smiled wanly at her approach. A bulky, red-tinged bandage covered the left side of his face from cheekbone to scalp. *He's alive! Thank God!*

"Honey, I forgot to duck."

"Quoting Ronald Reagan in a blue state, darling?"

"Why not? I'm playing the hero's best friend."

"What happened?"

"A delicate question," Rep said, using a minimal nod to draw Fletcher and Cyclops to Melissa's attention.

"He crowded me so I cold-cocked him," Hoeckstra said with a verbal shrug. "I had no idea who he was. I didn't think I hit him all that hard. I just wanted to discourage him a little."

Melissa pivoted with an athleticism she hadn't deployed since high school soccer and slapped Hoeckstra across the face as hard as she could.

"Cyclops!" Fletcher barked. "Chick fight!"

This prediction proved optimistic, at least from Fletcher's viewpoint. Hoeckstra flinched reflexively at the smack and grunted in pain as her left cheek flattened under Melissa's stinging palm, but she made no effort to avoid the slap or retaliate for it.

"Okay, that makes us even. The next one's gonna cost you."

Ignoring the threat, Melissa turned back to the gurney.

"Concussion?" she asked.

"For sure," said a crusty med tech who had ex-Navy-Pharmacist's-Mate stamped unmistakably on his features. "He'll need some stitches, but he'll be all right after a night in the hospital."

"Actually," Rep said as he began to push himself up from the gurney, "I think I can get in for those stitches under my own steam."

"Like hell you will," the med tech said, shoving him back down. "I'm taking you for a ride."

"Doesn't that require my consent?"

"Sue me."

"Just a minute, then," Rep said. He extracted a folded sheet of printer paper from his inside coat pocket and handed it to Melissa. "This is for you."

Although she already knew what it was, Melissa unfolded the paper and examined it. Murmuring "Interesting," she showed it to Clevenger and Hoeckstra:

MELISSA SETON PENNYWORTH

From:	Pennyworth, Melissa [msp@uwm.edu]
Sent:	Wednesday, 04 Feb 08 13:12
To:	Lt. Cmdr. Francis X. Seton
	[lcdrfxetonusna@navy.mil]
Subject:	Meeting

Bro,

Rep will be at the church, but say a prayer for me anyway if you have time. It can't hurt.

'Lissa

"I don't understand," Hoeckstra said.

"Don't understand what?" Clevenger asked.

"Look at the 'Sent' line," Hoeckstra said. "Pennyworth's email printer for some reason uses military notation to show date and time. '4 February' instead of 'February 4,' and a twenty-four hour clock instead of a.m. and p.m. Thirteen-twelve means twelve minutes past thirteen-hundred hours—in other words, one-twelve p.m. But one-twelve p.m. was a few minutes ago, while we were chatting in church and the invalid here was taking a nap in the snow."

"Well, obviously," Clevenger said, "she wrote the email to her brother just over an hour ago. He printed it out at the Naval Academy, where the print-out showed eastern standard time in military notation. Then he faxed it to Mr. Pennyworth, and what we have here is the facsimile."

"Except that that's not what happened," Rep said. "Melissa sent the email at twelve minutes after noon, Milwaukee time, just as you said. It was the last thing she did before she left for Saint Josephat's. But I printed it out myself from our computer a few minutes later, before I left to come here."

"If you printed it out in Milwaukee, and it was sent from Milwaukee, why does it show the 'Sent' time in military format and Eastern Standard Time?" Hoeckstra asked.

"Because I sent it to a military installation in Annapolis, Maryland," Melissa said. "A few days ago I printed out an email that Frank had sent me *from* the Naval Academy. *That* email showed the 'Sent' time in standard notation instead of military, and it showed central standard instead of eastern standard time. If you print out an email you've sent using Outlook software, it uses the time and date format of the person you sent it to, not yours. And it shows the time at the recipient's location, not your location, as the time the email was sent."

"Wait a minute!" Hoeckstra turned to confront Clevenger. "That means the email they found on Angstrom doesn't give you an alibi for his murder after all. You could have printed it out yourself in Chicago after he had already left South Bend.

South Bend, Indiana is on eastern time and Chicago is on central. Because the email was sent to an email address in South Bend, the print-out would show eastern standard time instead of central standard time even though you printed it in Chicago. Then you could have planted it on him when you killed him."

"She has a point," Melissa said. "The email made it look like you were with me at the time he had to have been killed. But an email sent to someplace in the eastern time zone will show eastern time regardless of where it was sent from or where it's printed out. Therefore, Angstrom didn't have to print that email off in South Bend. If you did what Hoeckstra just said, you would have had enough time to kill Angstrom and plant the email on him before you and I got together."

"'Could' ain't 'did,'" Clevenger said in a surprisingly mild voice. "After all, it was pure happenstance that his body was found while I was still in your company. It might not have been found for three days. If that had happened, given the imprecision of estimates about time of death, my meeting with you wouldn't have proven anything. I could have killed him after you and I had parted company. If I were trying to fabricate an alibi, I wouldn't have left the discovery of the body to luck."

"I don't think you did leave it to luck," Melissa said. "I haven't forgotten the cigarette break you took during our conversation at Spirits of Chicago. Did you go out on the terrace late on a frigid afternoon to call in an anonymous tip about a body in a Prius in the hotel parking ramp instead of to smoke a Dunhill? You made it a point to stay in my sight, you talked on a cell-phone, and you don't seem all that fanatical about smoking."

"If I'd done that, the police could trace the nine-one-one call to my number."

"Not if you used a throwaway phone with prepaid minutes—which is what you accused Hoeckstra of doing to set up our meeting today."

"*I* didn't set any meeting up," Hoeckstra said indignantly to Clevenger. "*You* left a message for *me*."

All three of them paused for a moment as a police car with flashing red and blue lights pulled up and a cop jumped out. Ignoring the trio of women, he stepped toward the gurney.

"Excuse me for bringing up a technicality," Clevenger said as the cop squatted down next to Rep and began exchanging comments with the med-tech, "but exactly why am I supposed to have killed Angstrom? He claimed to have evidence that would have helped my son's case. I wanted him alive, not dead."

"He did have that evidence," Melissa said, "but you didn't need to buy it from him. You already knew what it was and how to document it."

"What are you talking about now?" Hoeckstra demanded.

"The research Professor Angstrom did for a corporate history of your family's company had turned up something interesting," Melissa told Hoeckstra. "Ms. Clevenger had gotten the company out of a legal scrape by talking Assistant United States Attorney Finnegan into recommending that charges not be pursued."

"That was just good lawyering," Clevenger said.

"That particular negotiation was part of a rather suggestive pattern. When your regulatory practice collapsed, you decided to re-invent yourself overnight as a credible white-collar crime specialist. You accomplished that by disclosing confidential information you had about some of your former clients to Finnegan. He got glossy prosecutions of high profile defendants; you got people who needed your services. In exchange, he gave you favorable deals for some of the targets who had the good sense to retain you. Outstanding results equal instant credibility."

"I told you so," Fletcher muttered to Cyclops. "That's the same kind of 'business development' that got Q in front of a jury this morning. She created the problems for her clients and then her clients hired her to fix them—just like Q did. Crime in the streets meets crime in the suites."

"But that would have been an incredible risk for Finnegan," Clevenger scoffed. "I would have had something to hold over him for the rest of his life."

"You were facing a much greater risk than he was," Melissa said. "Rep tells me that it's not even clear Finnegan was doing anything wrong. The attorney-client privilege doesn't keep cops from talking to whistle-blowers. Potential defendants turn state's evidence all the time, and prosecutors make deals with them. If you or anyone else had disclosed your role, though, you would certainly have been disbarred. Your career would have been over."

"Wait a minute," Hoeckstra said. "How would any of this legal insider stuff have helped her brat? It's got nothing to do with whether he threatened to rape me. I don't see how it could even have been admitted at trial."

"It might not have been," Rep said. "But it could have been used to force Finnegan off the case. Once some prosecutor without his own political agenda was handling the case, any good defense lawyer could have made a decent deal to get rid of it."

"You knew it was potentially devastating evidence that could save your son," Melissa said to Clevenger. "You described it conceptually to the defense team. That's why they included it in the material they used with the mock jury. But when push came to shove, you weren't willing to put your career in jeopardy even to save Jimmy. You would have let Jimmy go to prison to save your own skin."

"You're missing something," Clevenger said. "Something rather big. If I already had the evidence, why would Angstrom think he could sell it to me?"

"He didn't. What he thought he could sell to you was his silence about it—his agreement not to expose you. He tried to blackmail you with that threat before the first trial, but you wouldn't bite. He had Tereska Bleifert plant the incriminating file in the press room during the trial. She thought she was doing it as a noble service to truth and justice, but Angstrom's real reason was to show you that he meant business. Unfortunately for him, though, Rep stumbled over the file the reporters were supposed to find. He not only didn't disclose it, he gave the documentation back to the company so that Angstrom didn't have it any more."

"And so I therefore supposedly killed Angstrom?" Clevenger asked.

"Yes. With the outcome on the appeal of Jimmy's case looking shaky, you suggested that Angstrom combine business with pleasure and come to Chicago for a roll in the hay with you and some wheeling and dealing over compromising information that he still had in his head, even if he couldn't document it."

"And then I somehow persuaded him to swallow curare?"

"Right, by putting it in a spray bottle with breath freshener and telling the old satyr to use it in preparation for the amorous adventure you promised him."

"In a cheap paperback novel your guesswork about a corrupt bargain with Finnegan would make me blurt out a tearful confession, if it were true," Clevenger said. "But it's not true, I'm not confessing, and your speculation proves nothing."

"It's not entirely guesswork. Everything I just said is in an offer of proof that was handed to Terry Finnegan two weeks ago. He hasn't thrown it back in anyone's face yet—and if it were nonsense I think he would have. Testimony from him could prove every word I just said."

For just a moment, the color in Clevenger's face turned a shade paler and her features showed the unpleasant surprise Melissa imagined seeing on Jane Austen's face when a deuce of trumps covered an ace during whist. She quickly recovered and when she spoke her tone was dismissive.

"Well, this is all very interesting, but the bottom line is that it's perfectly asinine. I said it isn't true, and I'll stick with that. You may have an outline for a retro *Thin Man* movie but you don't have evidence and you aren't going to gin any up by trying a lame bluff on Finnegan."

"Rule four-oh-four-b," Rep said to Clevenger.

"Four-*zero*-four," Hoeckstra said to Rep.

"Please do shut up," Melissa said to Hoeckstra.

"What?" Clevenger said to Rep.

"*Modus operandi*," Rep said. "Plan and preparation. One of the exceptions to the rule against introducing evidence of prior bad acts of the defendant in a criminal case."

"Interesting academic point," Clevenger said, "but unless you actually *have* the evidence in the first place, that's all it is. Save it for a law review article. Now, if anyone needs me, I'll be at my office, practicing law."

She turned away and began cutting through the crowd on the way to her car. She nodded politely at the cop on her way.

"As long as we're throwing Latin around," Melissa called, reaching into her purse, "there's something you might want to watch, just for chain of custody purposes. Officer?"

Clevenger turned around with a puzzled expression. The officer, equally baffled, stood up and swiveled toward Melissa. Melissa took a small bottle of Chloraseptic analgesic throat spray from her purse. She handled it carefully, holding it on the top and bottom with the tips of her thumb and index finger. This time Clevenger's face paled by much more than a shade. Her lips fell open. White puffs of breath came rapidly until she was almost panting.

"I'd like you to verify that I'm handing this spray bottle that I just took from my purse to an officer of the Milwaukee Police Department," Melissa said. "You're welcome to examine my purse to confirm that there aren't any other spray bottles in there if you like."

"What's that supposed to prove?" Hoeckstra asked.

"Nothing, if Ms. Clevenger is telling the truth." Melissa dropped the bottle into the officer's palm. "But if the contents of that bottle turn out to be laced with poison, it might suggest that when she knocked my purse on the church floor a few minutes ago and picked it up, she substituted poisoned spray for the stuff I've been ostentatiously using in her presence."

"What does she have against you?" Hoeckstra demanded. "I mean, aside from your obnoxiously superior attitude?"

"If I had to speculate, I'd guess that Taylor Gates told her that I thought the same person who murdered Angstrom was also responsible for the death of Timothy Goettinger. That started her worrying that if I kept on poking my nose into things I might stumble onto something she'd find inconvenient."

"Murdered my father?" Hoeckstra shrieked.

"Angstrom wasn't the first person to threaten Clevenger with disclosure," Melissa said. "Timothy Goettinger was obsessively investigating his company's unprecedented involvement with the criminal justice system. He didn't blame Clevenger for it, or suspect that she was implicated in any wrongdoing, but his investigation threatened to bring out her cozy arrangement with Finnegan. He was old school, a man of integrity and rigid principles. Whatever he found, he was going to go public with it."

"That sounds like dad, all right," Hoeckstra said. "But how do you know those details? Is that guesswork too?"

"No. There had to be documentation of at least that much. Otherwise, the file Rep gave back to the company wouldn't have been scary enough to force a six-figure settlement."

"Tim Goettinger wasn't poisoned," Clevenger said. "He died of a heart condition diagnosed years before at Columbia by one of the top cardiac specialists in the country."

"A condition that was being effectively controlled by medication, but that would cause a marked physical deterioration if someone substituted placebos for the pills he was supposed to be taking—like poison being substituted for my throat spray."

"Which his mistress could have done," Hoeckstra said, her voice eerily quiet now instead of angry or hysterical.

"I wasn't his mistress, I was his *lover*," Clevenger spat. "I cried my eyes out when he died. And I certainly didn't kill him."

"I don't think you were trying to kill him," Melissa said. "You just wanted to send him to the doctor, who'd send him to the hospital, thinking that his heart condition was getting worse. You figured that would distract him from his investigation into your adventures with Finnegan. But hearts are unpredictable, and when Angstrom lured him to an unused confessional at Saint Josephat's to pick up a file he thought was compromising enough to produce a payoff, Goettinger's heart gave out."

"And I just happened to be there."

"You had to follow him around as his condition deteriorated, because when he collapsed you'd need to retrieve the placebos left in his medicine bottle and replace them with the real medication that you'd been secreting."

"That all sounds pretty far-fetched to me."

"Just ask Rep. I replaced the medication in several of our Contac cold capsules with sugar. It took some effort, but I got it done."

"You apparently did," Rep said. "I have a whole new understanding of the term 'placebo effect.'"

"Well," Clevenger said, "I didn't do anything of the kind."

"Yes you did."

The flat assertion came from the edge of the crowd, and everyone's head turned to see Bleifert, who had been milling unnoticed in the group for several minutes. She fumbled nervously with a St. Joseph's Missal—a prayer book slightly smaller than a brick and just as hard, with all the readings for the entire three-year cycle of Sunday and weekday masses. She took a deep breath and continued.

"Professor Pennyworth asked me to come here today. She promised she wouldn't tell anyone else I was here. It would be up to me to decide whether to come forward."

"Tell us what you saw, young lady," the cop rumbled.

"When I saw Ms. Clevenger come out of the confessional this afternoon, it was like *déjà vu*. I had seen it before—the day Mr. Goettinger died. Except that time she brought a file out with her. Seeing her this afternoon makes me certain she was the one I saw that day."

Clevenger paused, looking without apparent concern from Bleifert to Hoeckstra to Melissa. She seemed completely composed.

"I've had enough nonsense for one afternoon," she said. Again she turned away.

"You sonofabitch!" Hoeckstra yelled, with a fine disregard for gender-neutral language. Her right hand reached for her parka pocket.

"Gun!" Rep yelled.

For a potentially fatal moment, with Rep's vicious wound vivid in her mind, Melissa found herself frozen by fear. By the time she could summon the will to leap forward, Hoeckstra was raising the gun and Melissa was sure she'd be too late. The cop was rushing forward, yelling "No! No! No!" but he was still ten feet away.

Hoeckstra had nearly leveled the Luger when a maroon blur whizzed through the air. Bleifert's missal smacked the right side of Hoeckstra's face. With a startled yelp Hoeckstra staggered backward. Her right hand jerked up and the Luger fired harmlessly into the air. Before she could regain her balance the cop had her in a hammerlock and the Luger lay in the snow, under his foot.

"What was that?" Clevenger demanded.

"The missile was a missal," Melissa said. "You were saved by a homonym."

"Why did you do that, you kraut-bitch?" Hoeckstra yelled at Bleifert as she writhed in the cop's arms. "She's not worth saving."

"I'm not a kraut-bitch, I'm a *polack*-bitch," Bleifert said. "And if your aim is as bad as your theology, she wasn't in much danger anyway."

"Hold it," the cop barked over Hoeckstra's shoulder at Clevenger, who was still moving steadily away, "you toddle on back. You four ladies and I are going down to the Safety Building to chat with guys in suits."

As unobtrusively as he could, which wasn't very, Cyclops replaced the long telephoto lens on his camera with a much shorter one that Rep guessed was about eighty-five millimeters. He raised it and bracketed the lens on the converging women.

"Skip the professor," Fletcher told him. "Shoot the lawyer twice."

Chapter Thirty-five

The Third Tuesday in March, 2008

"Terry feels strongly about this prosecution," Maria Sanchez said.

"Should I be talking to Terry or should I be talking to you?" Kuchinski asked, feigning grumpiness.

"I'm lead counsel now. Terry has recused himself to avoid any appearance of impropriety."

"Well I think that's just not fair. If Terry's gonna stick you with a dead horse in a bathtub for a case and then not let you run it yourself, he at least oughta come into court and take the beating with you."

"I'm running the case. And it's the same case that pulled eleven jurors last time around."

"Fortunately for our side, you need twelve." Kuchinski took a large manila envelope from his briefcase and worried the flap up. "And it's not the same case. We'll have some evidence this time that first jury didn't see."

"Don't bother. My complaining witness took a shot at the defendant's mother. I know. I saw it in the paper. Since mom might be facing murder charges in two states before long, I kind of like our side of that one."

Kuchinkski's eyes glinted as a mordant smile split his lips. He pulled out three eight-by-tens and splayed them across

Sanchez's desk. He pointed at the top-center of the first one, where Hoeckstra's forearm was driving into Rep.

"You didn't see *this* set of glossies in the paper. I particularly like this one. See the way she has her knees bent just right, so she can explode up and out through her legs and hips? If the Packers could get their guards to block like that they might have a running game next season."

"So she's a strong woman. Juries like that."

"Point is, she's too strong to be scared of my client, who's your basic lover-not-a-fighter type."

"I can't blow off an attempted rape because the victim beat up a lawyer."

"What I'm thinking," Kuchinski said musingly, "is misdemeanor disorderly conduct, no 'sex offender' tag on his forehead, no prison time, unsupervised probation, and four-hundred hours of community service."

"No way he's getting off with three months of emptying bedpans," Sanchez snapped. "That pampered punk—"

Her phone rang. She glanced at the caller's number, raised her eyebrows apologetically, mouthed "I have to take this," and picked up the receiver. Ten seconds later she looked like she'd drawn to a busted flush and was trying to hide it. Thirty seconds after that, with the silence broken only by a "yes" or "got it" or "right" now and then, she looked like she'd taken a gut punch after a Tex-Mex buffet. She hung up and as she turned her face back to Kuchinski she seemed to be trying to come up with the right words to say something.

"Clevenger cashed in her chips, didn't she?" Kuchinski asked, reading the younger lawyer like a West Digest headnote.

"Waded into Lake Michigan with her pockets full of Smartbelle walking weights. Her body washed up on the beach a little over an hour ago. If the tide had been going out instead of in she might not have been found for weeks."

"She probably didn't leave that to chance."

"Probably not." Sanchez's voice was weary and dull.

"I'm guessing there's a note mentioning this prosecution."

"I didn't get those details," Sanchez said.

"You need some time to digest this?" Kuchinski asked.

His words and his tone were thoughtful and sensitive, but predation gleamed in his cold blue eyes. He was really asking Sanchez if she were tough enough to handle the situation, and both of them knew it.

"No," she said, and then repeated, "No," as if the answer required confirmation.

"A pampered punk is one thing. A grieving orphan—well, I might could do something with that."

"I know that. Look. Make it six-hundred hours of community service and no drugs or alcohol during the probation, and if the victim consents I'll recommend it."

Chapter Thirty-six

The Fourth Saturday in March, 2008

"Thank you all for coming," Bleifert said to the cluster of people scattering from the porch outside St. Josephat's. "And especially thank you, Mr. Pennyworth. I know this isn't your religious tradition. It was very thoughtful of you to join us."

Rep glanced at the people now trudging away: Jimmy Clevenger, Father Huebner, Terry Finnegan, Kuchinski, and a couple of UWM students.

"I'm pretty eclectic," Rep said. "I'm one of those 'a prayer is a prayer' types. And seeing you produce eight people to pray in a Catholic church for an atheist who committed suicide was worth the price of admission all by itself."

"The way she killed herself left her time to repent even after she was under water," Bleifert said. "All things are possible with God. After all, Saint Dismis was a career criminal who saved his soul in the last hour of his life."

"Saint Dismis was the thief who was crucified beside Christ," Melissa said in response to Rep's blank look.

"Well, thanks again. I'll see you on Monday, I guess." Hands buried in the pockets of her jacket, Bleifert nodded and walked away.

"I guess that's that," Rep said.

"Smiles don't come easily to her and she managed one," Melissa said as they began walking toward their Taurus. "Give her credit for that."

"I give her credit for a lot more than that. I meant what I said. But please tell me that you don't buy the eleventh-hour conversion theory."

"I think Clevenger was a pagan who died a pagan's death. When push came to shove, though, she gave her life to save her son."

"You got that part right," Rep said. "She knew exactly what she was doing when she walked into that lake. I'm not qualified to say whether it was a mortal sin, but it was certainly a first-rate litigation tactic."

Rep opened the driver's side door of their car and then clicked the button that opened the passenger door for Melissa. Before he slid behind the wheel he gave her a long and intrigued look over the car's roof.

"I noticed that you didn't genuflect when we left church. I'd been wondering whether you were like some of those con-men who fall in love with their spiels and end up buying into their own scams. I thought maybe you were so convincing when you told Tereska about feeling drawn back to the Church that you ended up believing it. Since you didn't genuflect, though, I'm surmising that Tereska's prayers for you haven't been answered yet."

"Yesterday was Good Friday, dear," Melissa said, her green-flecked brown eyes glinting. "The altar was stripped after Holy Thursday services. The tabernacle is empty, to symbolize Christ in the tomb. Even for the most dogmatic Catholic in the world, genuflecting in church today wouldn't make any more sense than genuflecting in our condo's entryway."

"Beloved," Rep said, as if he'd caught her elbow-deep in the cookie jar, "you've been brushing up."

"Busted." She blushed and grinned.

End Note

The headlines cited during the colloquy at Villa Terrace are actual quotations from the referenced newspapers and other sources cited. See J. Bottum and D. Dalin (eds.), *The Pius War*, 108-109 (Lexington Books 2004).

To receive a free catalog of Poisoned Pen Press titles, please contact us in one of the following ways:

Phone: 1-800-421-3976
Facsimile: 1-480-949-1707
Email: info@poisonedpenpress.com
Website: www.poisonedpenpress.com

Poisoned Pen Press
6962 E. First Ave. Ste. 103
Scottsdale, AZ 85251